THE RAIN GOD

THE RAIN GOD

A Desert Tale

ARTURO ISLAS

ALEXANDRIAN PRESS
PALO ALTO

Published in 1984 by Alexandrian Press
678 Mirada Avenue
Stanford, California 94305
Printed in the United States of America

Designed by James Stockton and Associates

Library of Congress Cataloging in Publication Data
Islas, Arturo, 1938-
  The rain god.
  I. Title. PS3559.S44R3 1984 813'.54 84-12323
ISBN 0-916485-00-5
ISBN 0-916485-01-3 (pbk.)

For my family — Jovita, Arturo,
Mario, and Luis

I come to speak through your dead mouths . . .
Give me silence, water, hope.
Give me struggle, iron, volcanoes.
Fasten your bodies to me like magnets.
Hasten to my veins, to my mouth.
Speak through my words and my blood.

Pablo Neruda

THE RAIN GOD

JUDGMENT DAY

A photograph of Mama Chona and her grandson Miguel Angel—Miguel Chico or Mickie to his family—hovers above his head on the study wall beside the glass doors that open out into the garden. When Miguel Chico sits at his desk, he glances up at it occasionally without noticing it, looking through it rather than at it. It was taken in the early years of World War II by an old Mexican photographer who wandered up and down the border town's main street on the American side. No one knows how it found its way back to them, for Miguel Chico's grandmother never spoke to strangers. She and the child are walking hand in hand. Mama Chona is wearing a black ankle-length dress with a white lace collar and he is in a short-sleeved light-colored summer suit with short pants. In the middle of the street life around them, they are looking straight ahead, intensely preoccupied, almost worried. They seem in a great hurry. Each has a foot off the ground, and Mama Chona's black hat with the three white daisies, their yellow centers like eyes that always out-stared him, is tilting backward just enough to be noticeable. Because of the look on his face, the child seems as old as the woman. The camera has captured them in flight from this world to the next.

Uncle Felix, Mama Chona's oldest surviving son, began calling the boy "Mickie" to distinguish him from his father Miguel Grande, a big man whose presence dominated all family gatherings even though he was Mama Chona's youngest son. Her name was Encarnacion Olmeca de Angel and she instructed everyone in the family to call her "Mama Grande" or "Mama Chona" and never, ever to address her as *abuelita*, the Spanish equivalent to granny. She was the only grandparent Miguel Chico knew. The others had died many years before he was born on the north side of the river, a second generation American citizen.

Thirty years later and far from the place of his birth, on his own deathbed at the university hospital, Miguel Chico, who had been away from it for twelve years, thought about his family and especially its sinners. Felix, his great-aunt Cuca, his cousin Antony on his mother's side—all dead. Only his aunt Mema, the pariah of the family after it initially refused to accept her illegitimate son, was still alive. And so was his father, Miguel Grande, whose sins the family chose to ignore because it relied on him during all crises.

Miguel Chico knew that Mama Chona's family held contradictory feelings toward him. Because he was still not married and seldom visited them in the desert, they suspected that he, too, belonged on the list of sinners. Still, they were proud of his academic achievements. He had been the first in his generation to leave home immediately following high school after being admitted to a private and prestigious university before it was fashionable or expedient to accept students from his background.

Mama Chona did not live to see him receive his doctorate and fulfill her dream that a member of the Angel family become a university professor. On her deathbed, surrounded by her family, she recognized Miguel Chico and said, *la familia*, in an attempt to bring him back into the fold. Her look and her words gave him that lost, uneasy feeling he had whenever any of his younger cousins asked him why he had not married. Self-consciously, he would say, "Well, I had this operation," stop there, and let them guess at the rest.

Miguel Chico, after he survived, decided that others believed the thoughts and feelings of the dying to be more melodramatic than they were. In his own case, he had been too drugged to be fully aware of his condition. In the three-month decline before the operation that would save his life, and as he grew thirstier every day, he longed to return to the desert of his childhood, not to the family but to the place. Without knowing it, he had been ill for a very long time. After suffering from a common bladder infection, he was treated with a medication that cured it but aggravated a deadly illness dormant since childhood though surfacing now and again in fits of fatigue and nausea.

"You didn't tell me you had a history of intestinal problems," the doctor said, leafing back through his chart.

"You didn't ask me," Miguel Chico replied. "And anyway, isn't it right there on the record?" He had lost ten pounds in two weeks and was beginning to throw up everything he ate.

"Well, I can't treat you for this now. I've cured your urinary infection. You'll have to go to a specialist at the clinic for the other. And stop taking the medication I prescribed for you." Later Mickie learned that no one with his history of intestinal illness ought to take the medication the doctor had prescribed. By then, it was too late.

He was allowed only spoonfuls of ice once every two hours and the desert was very much in his mouth, which was already parched by the drugs. Not at the time, but since, he has felt his godmother Nina's fear of being buried in the desert. Those chips of ice fed to him by his brother Raphael were grains of sand scratching down his throat. In the last weeks before surgery, as he lost control over his body, he floated in a perpetual dusk and, had it happened, would have died without knowing it, or would have thought it was happening to someone else.

There was one moment when he sensed he might not live. As the surgeon and anesthetist lifted him off of the gurney and onto the hard, cold table, each spoke quietly about what they were going to do. Mickie heard their voices, tender and kind, and was impressed by the way they touched him—as if he were a person in pain. He thought in those seconds that if theirs were the last voices he was to hear, that would be fine with him, for he longed to escape from the drugged and disembodied state of twilight in which he had lived for weeks. His uncle Felix had been murdered in such a twilight.

The doctors set him down and uncovered him. He weighed ninety-eight pounds and looked pregnant.

"Your mother is waiting just outside," said the surgeon's voice at his right ear.

"I'm going to relax you a little bit so that this tube won't hurt your nose or throat," said the anesthetist at his left.

Someone began shaving his abdomen and loins. "God, is he hairy," said a nurse loudly.

Miguel Chico did not care whether or not he survived the operation they planned for him. When they described it to him and told him he would have to wear a plastic appliance at his side for the rest of his life—a life, they were quick to assure him, which would be perfectly "normal"— they grinned and added, "It's better than the alternative."

"How would you know?" he asked. "Let me die."

Thus, at first he was considered a difficult patient. Later on, the drugs seeped through, drop by drop, and conquered his rebelliousness. When the nurses came in to check on him every twenty minutes and to ask him how he felt, "Just fine," he would answer, even as he watched himself piss, shit, and throw up blood. Only later, when he survived ("It's a miracle," the surgeon told his mother, "his intestine was like tissue paper"), forever a slave to plastic appliances, did he see how carefully he had been schooled by Mama Chona to suffer and, if necessary, to die.

Lying on a gurney in the recovery room, Miguel Chico came to life for the second time. Tubes protruded from every opening of his body except his ears, and before he was able to open his eyes, he heard a woman's voice calling his name over and over again in the way that made him wince: "Mee-gwell, Mee-gwell, wake up, Mee-gwell." Another voice from inside his head kept saying, "You cannot escape from your body, you cannot escape from your body."

He opened his eyes. In the gurney next to his there appeared a fat, strawberry blonde on all fours screaming for something to kill the pain inside her head. "Nurse, give me something for my head!" she yelled without stopping. The nurse, this time a delicate Polynesian dressed in bright green and wearing a mask, glided in and out of his vision.

"Now, now, sweetheart," she said to the fat woman in a lovely, lilting voice, "you're going to be all right, and I'll bring you something in just a minute." She disappeared with a lithe, dreamy motion.

The fat woman was not appeased and she screamed more loudly than before. He wondered why she was on all fours if she had just come from surgery. Only later did it occur to him that he might have imagined her. At the time, she awakened him to his own pain.

Looking down at himself, he saw that his body was being held together by a network of tubes and syringes. On his left side, by the groin, the head of a safety pin gleamed. He could not move his lips to ask for water, and from neck to crotch his body felt like dry ice, the desert on a cold, clear day after a snowfall. If he had been able to move his arms, he would have pulled out the tubes in his nose and down his throat so that he, too, might shout out his horror and sense of violation. All of his needs were being taken care of by plastic devices and he was nothing but eyes and ears and a constant, vague pain that connected him to his flesh. Without this pain, he would have possessed for the first time in his life that consciousness his grandmother and the Catholic church he had renounced had taught him was the highest form of existence: pure, bodiless intellect. No shit, no piss, no blood—a perfect astronaut.

"I'm an angel," he said inside his mouth to Mama Chona, already dead and buried. "At last, I am what you taught us to be."

"Mee-gwell," sang the nurse, "wake up, Mee-gwell."

"It's Miguel," he wanted to tell her pointedly, angrily, "it's Miguel," but he was unable to speak. He was a child again.

They took him to the cemetery for three years before Miguel Chico understood what it was. At first, he was held closely by his nursemaid Maria or his uncle Felix. Later, he walked alongside his mother and godmother Nina or sometimes, when Miguel Grande was not working, with his father, holding onto their hands or standing behind them as they knelt on the ground before the stones. No grass grew in the poor peoples' cemetery, and the trees were too far apart to give much shade. The desert wind tore the leaves from them and Miguel Chico asked if anyone ever watered these trees. His elders laughed and patted him on the head to be still.

Mama Chona never accompanied them to the cemetery. "Campo Santo" she called it, and for a long time Miguel Chico thought it was a place for the saints to go camping. His grandmother taught him and his cousins that they must respect the dead, especially on the Day of the Dead when they wandered about the earth until they were remembered by the living. Telling the family that the dead she cared about were buried too far away for her to visit their graves, Mama Chona shut herself up in her bedroom on the last day of October and the first day of November every year for as long as she lived. Alone, she said in that high-pitched tone of voice she used for all important statements, she would pray for their souls and for herself that she might soon escape from this world of brutes and fools and join them. In that time her favorite word was "brute," and in conversation, when she forgot the point she wanted to make, she would close her eyes, fold her hands in prayer, and say, "Oh, dear God, I am becoming like the brutes."

At the cemetery, Miguel Chico encountered no saints but saw only stones set in the sand with names and numbers on them. The grownups told him that people who loved him were there. He knew that many people loved him and that

9

he was related to everyone, living and dead. When his parents Miguel Grande and Juanita were married, his godmother Nina told him, all the people in the Church, but especially her, became his mothers and fathers and would take care of him if his parents died. Miguel Chico did not want them to die if it meant they would become stones in the desert.

They bought flowers that smelled sour like Mama Chona and her sister, his great-aunt Cuca, to put in front of the stones. Sometimes they cried and he did not understand that they wept for the dead in the sand.

"Why are you crying?" he asked.

"Because she was my sister" or "because she was my mother" or "because he was my father," they answered. He looked at the stones and tried to see these people. He wanted to cry too, but was able to make only funny faces. His heart was not in it. He wanted to ask them what the people looked like but was afraid they would become angry with him. He was five years old.

There were other people walking and standing and kneeling and weeping quietly in front of the stones. Most of them were old like his parents, some of them were as old as Mama Chona, a few were his own age. They bought the yellow and white flowers from a dark, toothless old man who set them out in pails in front of a wagon. Miguel shied away when the ugly little man tried to give him some flowers.

"Take them Mickie," said his godmother, "the nice man is giving them to you."

"I don't want them." He felt like crying and running away, but his father had told him to be a man and protect his mother from the dead. They did not scare him as much as the flower man did.

A year later, he found out about the dead. His friend

Leonardo, who was eight years old and lived in the corner house across the street, tied a belt around his neck. He put one end of the belt on a hook in the back porch, stood on a chair, and knocked it over. Nardo's sister thought he was playing one of his games on her and walked back into the house.

The next morning Miguel's mother asked if he wanted to go to the mortuary and see Leonardo. He knew his friend was dead because all the neighborhood was talking about it, about whether or not the boy had done it on purpose. But he did not know what a mortuary was and he wanted to find out.

When they arrived there, Miguel saw that everything was white, black, or brown. The flowers, like the kind they bought from the old man only much bigger and set up in pretty ways, were mostly white. The place was cold and all the people wore dark, heavy clothes. They were saying the rosary in a large room that was like the inside of the church but not so big. It was brightly lit and had no altar, but there were a few statues, which Miguel recognized. A long, shiny metal box stood at the end of the room. It was open, but Miguel was not able to see inside because it was too far away and he was too small to see over people's heads, even though they were kneeling.

Maria and his mother said that he must be quiet and pray like the others in the room. He became bored and sleepy and felt a great longing to look into the box. After the praying was over, they stood in line and moved slowly toward the box. At last he would be able to see. When the people in front of them got out of the way, he saw himself, his mother, and Maria reflected in the brightly polished metal. They told him it was all right to stand so that his head was level with theirs as they knelt. The three of them looked in.

11

Leonardo was sleeping, but he was a funny color and he was very still. "Touch him," his mother said, "it's all right. Don't be afraid." Maria took his hand and guided it to Nardo's face. It was cold and waxy. Miguel looked at the candles and flowers behind the box as he touched the face. He was not afraid. He felt something but did not know what it was.

"He looks just like he did when he was alive, doesn't he, Mickie?" his mother said solemnly.

"Yes," he nodded, but he did not mean it. The feeling was circling around his heart and it had to do with the stillness of the flowers and the color of Nardo's face.

"Look at him one more time before we go," Maria said to him in Spanish. "He's dead now and you will not see him again until Judgment Day."

That was very impressive and Miguel Chico looked very hard at his friend and wondered where he was going. As they drove home, he asked what they were going to do with Leonardo.

His mother, surprised, looked at Maria before she answered. "They are going to bury him in the cemetery. He's dead, Mickie. We'll visit him on the Day of the Dead. *Pobrecito, el inocente*," she said, and Maria repeated the words after her. The feeling was now in his stomach and he felt that he wanted to be sick. He was very quiet.

"Are you sad, Mickie?" his mother asked before saying goodnight to him.

"No."

"Is anything wrong? Don't you feel well?" She put her hand on his forehead. Miguelito thought of his hand on Nardo's face.

"I'm scared," he said, but that was not what he wanted to say.

"Don't be afraid of the dead," his mother said. "They can't hurt you."

"I'm not afraid of the dead." He saw the sand and stones for what they were now.

"What are you afraid of, then?"

The feeling and the words came in a rush like the wind tearing the leaves from the trees. "Of what's going to happen tomorrow," he said.

The next day, Miguel Chico watched Maria comb her long beautiful black and white hair in the sun. She had just washed it, and the two of them sat on the backstairs in the early morning light, his head in her lap. Her face was wide, with skin the color and texture of dark parchment, and her eyes, which he could not see because as he looked up her cheekbones were in the way, he knew were small and the color of blond raisins. When he was very young, Maria made him laugh by putting her eyes very close to his face and saying in her uneducated Spanish, "Do you want to eat my raisin eyes?" He pretended to take bites out of her eyelids. She drew back and said, "Now it's my turn. I like your chocolate eyes. They look very tasty and I'm going to eat them!" She licked the lashes of his deeply set eyes and Miguel Chico screamed with pleasure.

Maria was one of hundreds of Mexican women from across the border who worked illegally as servants and nursemaids for families on the American side. Of all ages, even as young as thirteen or fourteen, they supported their own families and helped to rear the children of strangers with the care and devotion they would have given their own relatives had they been able to live with them. One saw these women standing at the bus stops on Monday mornings and late Saturday nights. Sunday was their only day off and most of them returned to spend it on the other side of the river.

In addition to giving her half of her weekly salary of twenty-five dollars, Juanita helped Maria pack leftover food, used clothing, old newspapers—anything Maria would not let her throw away—into paper bags that Maria would take to her own family. Years later, wandering the streets of New York, his own bag glued to his side, Miguel Chico saw Maria in all the old bag ladies waiting on street corners in Chelsea or walking crookedly through the Village, stopping to pick through garbage, unable to bear the waste of the more privileged.

"Now, Maria," Juanita said, "if the immigration officials ask you where you got these things, tell them you went to bargain stores."

"Si, señora."

"And if they ask you where you have been staying during the week, tell them you've been visiting friends and relatives. Only in emergencies are you to use our name and we'll come to help you no matter what it is."

"Si, señora."

The conversation was a weekly ritual and unnecessary because Miguel Grande through his police duties was known by immigration officials, who, when it came to these domestics, looked the other way or forgot to stamp cards properly. Only during political campaigns on both sides of the river were immigration laws strictly enforced. Then Maria and all women like her took involuntary vacations without pay.

Mama Chona did not approve of any of the Mexican women her sons and daughters hired to care for her grandchildren. They were ill educated and she thought them very bad influences, particularly when they were allowed to spend much time with her favorites. Mama Chona wanted Miguel Chico to be brought up in the best traditions of the Angel family. Juanita scoffed at those traditions. "They've eaten beans all their lives. They're no better than anyone else," she said to her sister Nina. "I'm not going to let my kids grow up to be snobs. The Angels! If they're so great, why do I have to work to help take care of them?"

Miguel Chico could not remember a time when Maria was not part of his family and even though Mama Chona disapproved of the way she spoke Spanish, she was happy to know that Maria was a devout Roman Catholic. She remained so the first six years of his life, taking him to daily mass and holding him in her arms throughout the services until he was four. After mass during the week and before he was old enough to be instructed by Mama Chona, Maria took him to the five-and-ten stores downtown. If she had saved money from the allowance Juanita gave her, she would buy him paper doll books. He and Maria spent long afternoons cutting out dolls and dressing them. When he got home from the police station, Miguel Grande would scold Maria for allowing his son to play with dolls. "I don't want my son brought up like a girl," he said to Juanita in Maria's presence. He did not like to speak directly to the Mexican women Juanita and his sisters took on to help them with the household chores. Miguel Chico's aunts Jesus Maria and Eduviges left notes for the "domestics" (the Spanish word *criadas* is harsher) and spoke to them only when they had not done their chores properly. Mama Chona had taught all her children that the Angels were better than the illiterate riff-raff from across the river.

"Maria does more good for people than all of them put together," Juanita complained to her sister and to her favorite brother-in-law Felix, who shared her opinion of his sisters. "They're so holier than thou. Just because they can read and write doesn't make them saints. I'd like to see them do half the work Maria does." Juanita knew that Jesus Maria

15

and Eduviges considered Felix's wife an illiterate and not worthy of their brother, who, after all, was an Angel.

"Apologize to your father for playing with dolls," Juanita said to Miguel Chico. He did but did not understand why he needed to say he was sorry. When his father was not there, his mother permitted him to play with them. She even laughed when Maria made him a skirt and they watched him dance to the jitterbug music on the radio. "Yitty-bog," Maria called it. Miguel Grande had caught them at that once and made a terrible scene. Again, Miguel Chico was asked to apologize and to promise that he would never do it again. His father said nothing to him but looked at Juanita and accused her of turning their son into a *joto*. Miguel Chico did not find out until much later that the word meant "queer." Maria remained silent throughout these scenes; she knew enough not to interfere.

After Miguel Chico's birthday, several months after his friend Leonardo "accidentally" hanged himself, Maria stopped taking him to mass. Instead, she spent the afternoons when he got home from school talking to him about God and reading to him from the Bible, always with the stipulation that he not tell his parents or Mama Chona. She especially liked to talk to him about Adam and Eve and the loss of paradise. He loved hearing about Satan's pride and rebelliousness and secretly admired him. Before he was expelled from the heavenly kingdom, Maria told him, Satan was an angel, the most favored of God's creatures, and his name was *Bella Luz*.

"Why did he turn bad, Maria?"

"Out of pride. He wanted to be God."

"Did God make pride?"

Miguel Chico learned that when he asked Maria a difficult question she would remain silent, then choose a biblical passage that illustrated the terrible power of God the Father's wrath. She loved to talk to him about the end of the world.

Maria began braiding her hair and tying it up in a knot that lay flat on her neck. It gave her a severe look he did not like, and he missed those mornings when she let her hair hang loosely to her waist and brushed or dried it in the sun, with his head on her lap. She did not allow him into her room any more and asked him to leave if he opened the door and caught her with her hair still unbraided. The word "vice" occurred frequently now in her talks with him; everything, it seemed, was becoming a vice to Maria. She had become a Seventh Day Adventist.

His mother and Maria got involved in long, loud, and tearful arguments about the nature of God and about the Catholic church as opposed to Maria's new religion. They excluded him from these discussions and refused to let him into the kitchen where they wrangled with each other and reached no conclusions. Miguel Chico hid in his mother's closet in order not to hear their shouting.

"The Pope is the anti-Christ!" Maria said loudly, hoping he would hear. And before Juanita could object, Maria cited a passage from the Bible as irrefutable proof.

"It's not true," Juanita said just as strongly, but she was not at ease with the holy book, and there was no priest at hand to back her up. She wept out of frustration and tried to remember what she had learned by rote in her first communion classes.

In the closet, Miguel Chico hugged his mother's clothes in terror. The familiar odors in the darkness kept him company and faintly reassured him. In the distance, the strident voices arguing about God continued. What would happen if he told his mother and father that Maria was sneaking him off to the Seventh Day Adventist services while they were away at work or having a good time? His father had said to his mother that he would kill Maria if she did that.

The services—which were not so frightening as his father's threats and the arguments between his mother and Maria—were held in a place that did not seem like a church at all it was so brightly lit up, even in the middle of the day. There were no statues and the air did not smell of incense and burning candles. The singing was in Spanish, not Latin, and it was not the sort he enjoyed because it reminded him of the music played in the newsreels about the war. The people at these services were very friendly and looked at him as if they all shared a wonderful secret. "You are saved," they would say to him happily. He did not know what they meant, but he sensed that to be saved was to be special. The more he smiled, the more they smiled back; they spent most of the time smiling, though they talked about things that scared him a great deal, such as the end of the world and how sinful the flesh was. He could not rid himself of the guilt he felt for being there, as no matter how much they smiled, he knew he was betraying his mother and father and Mama Chona in some deep, incomprehensible way.

The voices of the women he loved were farther away now, which meant they were almost finished for the time being and would soon resume their household chores. His mother had just given birth to a second son and was staying home from work to nurse him. They named him Gabriel and Miguel Chico was extremely jealous of him.

Opening the closet door after the voices had stopped altogether, Miguelito stumbled over the clothes hamper and some of his mother's things spilled out into the light. He saw an undergarment with a bloody stain on it. Quickly, he threw the clothes back into the basket and shoved it into the closet. He was careful not to touch the garment. Its scent held him captive.

Maria swept him up from behind, forcing him to laugh out of surprise, and trotted him into the kitchen. Together they stood looking out into the backyard through the screen door. It was a hot day and the sun made the screen shimmer. Miguel saw his mother bending over the verbena and snapdragons that she and Maria took great pains to make grow out of the desert. The flowers were at their peak, and already he knew that the verbena, bright red, small, and close to the ground, would outlast the more exotic snapdragons he liked better. The canna lilies, which formed the border behind them, were colorful, but they had no fragrance and were interesting only when an occasional hummingbird dipped its beak into their red-orange cups. In the corner of that bed grew a small peach tree that he had planted at Maria's suggestion from a pit he had licked clean two summers earlier. It was now a foot high and had branched. His mother was approaching it. Leaning over him and with her hand on his face directing his gaze toward the tree, Maria whispered hypnotically. "Look at the little tree," she said very softly in Spanish so that his mother could not hear. "When it blooms and bears fruit that means that the end of the world is near. Now look at your mother. You must respect and love her because she is going to die." In front of him, in the gauzy brightness of the screen, the red of the flowers merged with the red stain he had seen a few moments before. He believed Maria. In that instant, smelling her hair and feeling her voice of truth moist on his ear, love and death came together for Miguel Chico and he was not from then on able to think of one apart from the other.

Two years later, in a fit of terror because he knew the

world was going to end soon, he told his parents that Maria had been taking him to her church. His father threw her out of the house but allowed her to return a few weeks later on the condition that she say nothing about her religion to anyone while she lived in his house. The arguments stopped, and she no longer read to him from the Bible.

Maria treated him nicely, but she hardly spoke to him and spent more time caring for his brother. Once or twice Miguel Chico caught her looking at him sadly and shaking her head as if he were lost to her forever. One day after school, when he was feeling bold, he said, "If God knew that Satan and Adam and Eve were going to commit a sin, why did He create them?"

"You must not ask me such things," she replied, "I'm not allowed to talk to you about them."

It was a lame answer and he knew that in some important way, he had defeated her. He hated her now and hoped that she would leave them soon and return to Mexico. When, several months later, she did go away, he stayed at Mama Chona's house all day and did not say goodbye to her. Juanita was upset with him when he got home.

"Maria wanted to tell you goodbye. Why didn't you come home before she left?"

"I don't like her any more," he said. "I'm glad she's gone." But later that night he felt an awful loneliness when he thought about her hair and eyes.

Long after Miguel Chico had completed his education and given up all forms of organized religion, a few years after his operation and his decision to live alone in San Francisco, his mother wrote him a long letter about Maria's visit to the desert. It was her first and only one, for she had moved to California and joined a congregation there. Except for her hair, which was now completely white, his mother said that she looked exactly the same. Miguel Chico reread the last paragraphs of the letter while sitting at his desk, occasionally looking out to the garden. The fog had not yet burned away and the ferns and lobelia were a neon green and blue. "She took me back to the years when I was young and you were a little boy," his mother wrote.

She remembers all the things you did, even the long white dress she made for you and how you would dance and swirl around while she and I played your audience. She even got up and showed me how you danced! That surprised me because she still is very religious and I thought her church prohibited dancing.

She eats raw cabbage "for her mind," she says, carrots for her eyes, and turnips for her arthritis. She looks healthy enough to me, but according to her she has diabetes, arthritis, varicose veins, and bad eyesight.

One afternoon while I was resting, she cleaned all my flower beds. She still loves gardening. We took her across the river where she stayed a few days with a niece. Your father and I picked her up the following Tuesday on Seventh St. where she had called from a phone booth. She had walked through the worst parts of town completely unafraid, at least three miles.

She left on Thursday because it snowed on Wednesday, and I didn't want to let her go. I was very sad to see her leave because I thought as I saw her get on the bus that I might never see her again.

I hope she comes back, Mickie, so that I can take her to visit all the family. She remembered every one of the Angels but only talked to some of them and to your godmother on the phone. I wasn't driving or getting out much. She told me it was all right because she had come to be with me anyway.

Your brother Gabriel came over several times during her visit when he was able to get away from his duties at the parish. Would you believe that the first time he came and even though she knows he is a priest, Maria asked him when he was going to get married. I thought this was rude but I didn't say anything. Gabriel replied quite strongly, though, "No, thanks. I've seen what marriage does to many people in my parish."

She promised to come and see us later in the year. I hope so.

Later, on his birthday, he received a letter from Maria herself. It was written in the kind of Spanish his grandmother deplored and was sent from Los Angeles.

My Dear Miguelito,

With all my love I write you this letter to greet you and offer my congratulations. I have wanted for a long time to find out your address so that I might write to you. Your little mother told me that you had been very ill with a terrible sickness but that you are now well. I'm very glad.

Your *mamita* is very beautiful still and I love her very much because she is very friendly and does not look down on anyone. Your father and brother were also very kind to me so that I must tell you that a week with them seemed like a day.

In three days, you will celebrate your birthday. I am going toward old age, 79, and I plan to walk into my eighties. I wish you long life and good health. May God bless you and keep you well, so that when the Father comes in the clouds of the sky, He will take you and me with Him to live in paradise and joy in the kingdom He is preparing for those who love Him, think in His name and keep His commandments.

I send you a hug.

Maria L. v. de Sanchez

Write me.

He meant to respond to her note right away, believing himself to be free of her influence and her distortions of religion and vice. He put it off, telling himself he would write as soon as his academic duties were finished for the year. She visited him in dreams, her hair loose and white and streaming to the floor, her immense jaw frozen in a perpetual smile that was alternately loving and terrifying.

A month later, Juanita phoned him from the desert to tell him that Maria was dead. She had been knocked down by a car as she was leaving her church service in Los Angeles. The driver was drunk. A child by her side had been killed outright. Maria survived a night and a day in the hospital, surrounded by members of her congregation, talking with them until she fell into a coma. She had died on the anniversary of his operation.

"Well, the end of the world finally came for her," he said.

"Oh, Mickie, don't be so heartless," his mother said quietly.

"I'm not being heartless, Mother. She lived for the end of the world. Of course, it had to be some poor vice-ridden slob who caught up with her." In trying to joke about death with Juanita, he sensed that he was only making it worse for her.

"Well, anyway, I thought you would want to know," she said.

"Sure, Mom, and I'm sorry I sounded cold about it. I'm just tired of death and everything associated with it."

"Well, I'm going to have your brother celebrate a mass in her name. I know you don't believe in it, but I'm going to pray for her even if she did think we were all going to hell for being Catholics."

"You do what you need to, Mom. I'm going to look for peach trees in Golden Gate Park for her."

"What are you talking about? Are you trying to be funny again?"

"No, Mom. I'm dead serious. I'll tell you that story sometime."

He did not go to the park that day and did not think very much about Maria or the family in general. He and his therapist had decided that Sundays made him even more melancholy than usual because they were "family" days and he knew that though the park would be filled with all kinds of people, he would find himself drawn to the family groups, especially if there were old people among them.

Instead, he did his laundry in the washeteria around the corner where he knew he would be in the company of those people who lived alone in the neighborhood. They would not disturb each other except to ask for change and would read their Sunday papers in peace and isolation like that of the islands in the Baltic he loved visiting every summer. When he got back, he put away his clothes and began to prepare supper for himself. He chopped mushrooms, onions, garlic, and tomatoes for the spaghetti sauce he had perfected over the years. His secret was to add sugar, marsala, onion soup mix, and finally, one of the red chiles from the wreath his godmother gave him every Christmas and to let the concoction simmer off and on for two or three hours. Its flavor would improve throughout the week.

While the sauce was bubbling, he put on his favorite records and went to the bathroom to change his appliance. It was a weekly ritual which took him an hour, or a little more if the skin around the piece of intestine sticking out from his right side was irritated. Without the appliance and the bags he attached to it and changed periodically throughout each day, he knew he could not live. He had forgotten what it was like to be able to hold someone, naked, without having a plastic device between them. He wanted to ask Maria if, on Judgment Day, his body would rise from the grave in its condition before or after the operation. He was still feeling bitterness toward her and all people who thought like her because they seemed so literal and simpleminded. This time, the skin around the stoma looked all right and he finished the process before all the records had played out.

After supper, he tried to read in his study and found that he kept looking at the photograph in which he and Mama Chona are walking downtown. He had no photograph of Maria. In some vastly significant way, he felt he was still the child of these women, an extension of them, the way a seed continues to be a part of a plant after it has assumed its own form which does not at all resemble its origin, but which, nevertheless, is determined by it. He had survived severe pruning and wondered if human beings, unlike plants, can water themselves.

He was also beginning to see in his day-to-day life with the bag at his side that too many false notions surrounded people like him who have been given a reprieve. He did not automatically or necessarily see life more or less positively for almost having lost it. Nor did he come bearing insights from the other side of the grave to comfort and reassure those who have not yet been threatened.

He was still seeing people, including himself, as books. He wanted to edit them, correct them, make them behave differently. And so he continued to read them as if they were invented by someone else, and he failed to take into account their separate realities, their differences from himself. When people told him of their lives, or when he thought about his own in the way that is not thinking but a kind of reverie outside time, a part of him listened with care. Another part fidgeted, thought about something else or went blank, and wondered why once again he was being offered such secrets to examine. Later he found himself retelling what he had heard, arranging various facts, adding others, reordering time schemes, putting himself in situations and places he had never been in, removing himself from conversations or moments that didn't fit.

Most of the time his versions were happier than their "real" counterparts, and in making them so he was indulging in one of Mama Chona's traits that as a very young child— the child who was holding her hand forever in a snapshot— he loved most. Mama Chona was never able to talk about the ugly sides of life or people, even though she was surrounded by them. For her grandchildren she dressed up the unpleasant in sugary tales and convinced them that she believed what she was saying. Later, in his adolescence and while she still retained her wits, Miguel Chico hated her for this very trait, seeing it as part of the Spanish conquistador snobbery that refused to associate itself with anything Mexican or Indian because it was somehow impure. What, Miguel Chico asked himself, did she see when she looked in the mirror? As much as she protected herself from it, the sun still darkened her complexion and no surgery could efface the Indian cheekbones, those small very dark eyes and aquiline nose. By then, his cousins and he smiled at each other when she began telling her tales of family incidents and relatives long since dead and buried. By then, in their young adulthood, they knew the "truth" and were too self-involved in their educations away from her and the family to give her credit for trying to spare them the knowledge that she, too, knew it. Slowly, she slipped into her fairy-tale world—at least outwardly. "Oh, my dear Miguelito," she said to him just after his first year at the university, "you are going to be the best-educated member of this family."

Sitting at his desk, gazing at the garden, fixing that old photograph forever outside of time and far from where it was taken, he knew she had not called him "dear." Mama Chona did not use endearments with anyone in the family. How silent she had been even when she talked—silent like those pyramids he had finally seen in Teotihuacan built to pay tribute to the sun and moon. He had felt the presence of the civilizations that had constructed them and, as he climbed the steep, stone steps so conceived as to give him the impression that he was indeed walking into the sky, he had seen why those people, his ancestors, thought themselves gods and had been willing to tear out the hearts of others to maintain that belief. The feeling horrified him still.

And Mama Chona was still very much a part of him. Perhaps, he told himself, watching the first wisps of fog drift in over his garden, perhaps he had survived—albeit in an altered form, like a plant onto which has been grafted an altogether different strain of which the smelly rose at his side, that tip of gut that would always require his care and attention, was only a symbol—perhaps he had survived to tell others about Mama Chona and people like Maria. He could then go on to shape himself, if not completely free of their influence and distortions, at least with some knowledge of them. He believed in the power of knowledge.

His need to give meaning to the accidents of life had become even more intense, and he had not yet begun to laugh at that need. Years earlier, he had started out to be a brain surgeon but had found his pre-med courses lifeless and impossible. Literature had given him another way to examine the mind. He knew he was no poet like his cousin JoEl, the most sensitive member of the family. He, Miguel Chico, was the family analyst, interested in the past for psychological, not historical, reasons. Like Mama Chona, he preferred to ignore facts in favor of motives, which were always and endlessly open to question and interpretation. Yet unlike his grandmother and Maria, Miguel Chico wanted to look at motives and at people from an earthly, rather than otherworldly, point of view. He sensed he had a long way to go.

He walked out into the garden. The fog was in and thicker than usual in his part of the City. He knew that during the early hours of the day it would moisten and freshen all he had planted there. In the morning, before going to teach his classes, he would get rid of the petunias. Their purple velvet color was fading and they were now rangy and going to seed. Like a god, he would uproot them and discard them even after having loved and enjoyed them so much.

He felt Maria's hand on his face, her hair smelling of desert sage and lightly touching the back of his neck as she whispered in his ear. Every moment is Judgment Day and to those who live on earth, humility is a given and not a virtue that will buy one's way into heaven.

Miguel Chico left the garden, changed his bag, undressed and went to bed.

CHILE

M iguel Chico's godmother Nina was a practical woman. The otherworldly side of her came to the surface before her son's death, and she explored it with the care and precision she used to prepare the annual income tax accounts of various business firms in town.

Money and cards fascinated her and Fortune followed her, if not abundantly, certainly with cheer. But it was not until her children were well into adolescence that she looked casually over her shoulder one day and recognized a greater power smiling at her from behind Fortune's face. This same power that would take away her son began training her early on to endure, rather than resign herself to, the deprivation.

Nina had always been afraid to die. The very idea of being buried in the earth filled her heart with terror. No matter that she would be dead and insensate by that time, the funeral rites passed through in a silence as complete as that of the chrysanthemums surrounding her corpse, Nina knew she would feel the desert trickling down her throat, and that knowledge was unbearable to her. At best, it made her irritable and anxious during the many ordinary activities of her busy days; at worst, it caused her unalleviated fits of depression.

"I don't care what you say," Nina said to her sister Juanita, "I know I'm going to feel it."

"But how? You'll be dead. You won't feel anything," Juanita replied. She was disturbed by how much Nina had been drinking lately. To Miguel Chico's mother, more than one drink was too much. Juanita had known about Nina's fears for a long time. When they were children sleeping in the same bed, she would get Nina a glass of water in the middle of the night and distract her by singing the latest Mexican ballads until she went back to sleep. Years later, when their children were babies, their endless and elaborate card games allayed Nina's terror but did not get rid of it.

"Let me get another scotchito," Nina said as Juanita dealt out another hand of five hundred rummy.

"You're being ridiculous, Nina. Sit down and play."

It was not until she discovered the spirit world that Nina began to recognize that death might not exist as she imagined it in her terror. At the bi-weekly seances in the basement of her friends' Mexican food restaurant, her nose itching from the Aqua Velva they sprinkled into the air to induce serenity, Nina gradually became aware of two women waving at her from a strange and unknown region. They were about the same age and Nina saw with joy that one of the women was her sister Antonia, who had died in her late twenties. The other woman was her mother, who at twenty-nine had died giving birth to Nina. She awoke from her trance weeping, greatly relieved and peaceful, her initial skepticism about spiritualism gone forever. She did not see the women again, but the possibility that she might gave her courage and kept alive her faith in some kind of practical afterlife. "Imagine," she said to Juanita, "the two of them at the same age. They were like sisters, not like mother and daughter."

Juanita, more dominated by Church doctrine than was her younger sister, did not approve of these "spook" gatherings, though when she saw how effectively they helped Nina overcome her childhood fears she decided to overlook the heresy and defend her sister against the family's ridicule. Nevertheless, Juanita staunchly refused Nina's repeated invitations to join her in exploring the afterlife, even if she was secretly and guiltily attracted to it.

Nina's own humor, lively and persistent even during her moments of anxiety, grew and she was able to bring happiness to everyone except her own family. Her husband Ernesto and their three children could not understand or accept her enthusiasm for the impalpable, and they were jealous of her time away from them.

Ernesto, a silent and calm man, brought up to believe in the teachings of the Church, expressed his disdain by becoming even more quiet after she returned from one of her encounters with the spirits. When Nina tried to share with him her excitement, Ernesto asked her not to talk to him about such things. She honored his request because she loved and respected him for his already serene nature, and she sensed that his soul was more highly evolved than hers.

Ernesto Garcia was a hard-working, responsible man. The children adored him with an affection they did not extend to Nina. She had married him because he was honest and because she liked the way he laughed. Like her, he could lose his temper, but unlike her, he was able to recover it quickly and not bear grudges. He was as stubborn as she, but his obstinacy showed itself in the determined way he provided for his family without allowing himself to get into debt. For a man of Mexican origin, coming of age and marrying during the Depression, that was an accomplishment. Then, too, Ernesto was different from other men she knew. He was not given to bragging or lording it over others. From the start, she had recognized his superiority.

"Come on, Neto, just go to one meeting with me."

"No, and stop telling me about them." He refused her invitations without anger. From that time on, when anyone phoned for her while she was at a seance, Ernesto said, "She's with the spirits right now. But don't worry, when she gets home, I'll bring her back down to earth."

In this period, Anna, their oldest child, had stopped quarreling with her mother and was too preoccupied with her school activities and boyfriends to pay much heed to Nina's idiosyncrasies. Their youngest child, Cristina, was still too young to give her parents much trouble. But Nina and her son Antony, almost fifteen, were beginning to disagree with each other about everything in stubborn and exaggerated ways. Usually Ernesto sided with his wife in these arguments, but at times he wondered aloud if she were not living too much with her head in the clouds. When Ernesto took Tony's part against her, Nina felt betrayed.

"I live with three rams and a crab in this house," Nina said to Juanita, who did not understand astrology or accept it as valid. "I'm nothing but air. What can I do?" She cooked her chile jalapeño.

Only three people could eat it: their lifelong friend El Compa, her son, and herself. For the remainder of humanity, her green chile sauce was fire itself. "Ay, Nina, why do you make it so hot?" Juanita asked, exasperated. She did not like being left out, but she no longer made valiant attempts to taste the stuff. Her nose began watering the minute she walked into Nina's kitchen on those days when she toasted the chiles. Water, tortillas, bread and butter, aspirin and other remedies had not been able to calm Juanita's digestive tract after those times she had gamely swallowed a spoonful.

"I don't make it hot. Do I grow the chiles? I only choose them at the market like everybody else. How can I help it if they come out tasting like that after I prepare them?"

"But how can you eat it? It's going to kill you."

Nina laughed at her sister. "It will prepare me for the devil." In those days, she believed in the devil.

Juanita and Ernesto watched El Compa, Antony, and Nina eat the chile sauce as if it were chicken soup. The only evidence the two outsiders had of its power was in the tears the eaters shed without restraint as they said over and over like a rosary, "It's so good, it's so good."

"You're crazy," Ernesto said to them and went into the living room to read the afternoon paper. But Juanita stayed to the end and participated vicariously in their ability to enjoy the extremes in life.

"Let me tell you a joke I heard about chile," El Compa said one winter evening as they sat down to eat.

"Is it dirty?" Juanita asked.

"No, comadre, would I tell a dirty joke in front of you?"

"That's what my husband always says before he goes ahead and tells one."

"Leave him alone, Juanita. Go on, Compa, tell it. I love stories about chiles," Nina said with a little girl's smile on her face. She could be salacious without being obscene and Juanita watched her carefully because she wanted to learn that talent. Juanita's best friend Lola, who was married to El Compa, had the same skill.

"I'm not talking about that kind of chile," El Compa said. "I'm talking about the kind we're eating."

"Go on, get it over with," Tony said, resigned to having to listen to another bad joke.

"Well, there was this gringo who was in Mexico for the first time. At a restaurant he ordered a mole poblano that was real hot. I mean hot, hotter than this."

"Impossible," Nina said, offended.

"Well, almost, comadre. Anyway, the poor guy sat there awhile after he ate a couple of mouthfuls, flames coming out of his ears, and when he could talk he asked the waitress to come over to his table. She saw right away from his face what was wrong, and she brought him some ice cream. 'What good will that do?' the guy asked her. 'It'll help take away the burn,' she told him."

"It never worked for me," Juanita said.

"Well, the next day," El Compa went on.

"Here it comes, the corny punch line," Tony said.

"Shut up, both of you," Nina said.

"The next day, the gringo is sitting on the toilet, and you know what he is saying?"

"No, what?" Juanita asked, taken in once again by El Compa's charm.

" 'Come on, ice cream, come on!' "

"Ay, *pelado!*" Juanita said, blushing and enjoying herself immensely. Nina and Tony laughed at both of them.

Nina was the youngest child in her family. Her mother was Mexican, but her father was half French and half Mexican. Unable to accept the death of his wife, he had not forgiven Nina for destroying what he had loved most in the world. He died when Nina and Juanita were in their teens, and Nina had been secretly glad because she had resented her father's authoritarian ways. Unfortunately for her own children, that tendency to be uncompromisingly strict survived in her methods of disciplining them.

"You hit them too much," Juanita said to her when the children were almost adolescents. She knew she was breaking their agreement not to interfere in how they brought up their children.

"They've got to learn," Nina replied, "I can't stand spoiled brats."

"You sound just like Papá, Nina. I can't believe it."

Their father's oldest child, a brother they never knew, had died as an infant in San Francisco. Their parents had sailed north from the Mexican fishing village on the Pacific where they had met and married. Seeing his son's death as divine retribution for his having left Mexico, their father, a cigar maker, gradually moved his family toward the homeland, settling in an obscure New Mexican town first and finally in the Texas border town where his three daughters were born.

"So you see, Miguelito," Nina said to her godson, "that's why you live in San Francisco. Your uncle's spirit is still there. He would be over seventy years old now, unless of course he's learned his lessons and progressed farther into the spirit world. Look for him in the clouds, Mickie."

"Oh, Nina, you know I don't believe in those things. And they're not clouds. It's just plain fog." He was a graduate student at the time and was therefore a literal young man who took himself and others very seriously.

Antonia, the oldest sister and the aunt Miguel Chico never knew, was their father's favorite. She died of tuberculosis. Nina and Juanita nursed her at home for a time, then went to see her at the sanatorium every day for five years until her death. After they buried her, Nina did not go to another funeral until her own son was buried in the new cemetery at the outer edge of the desert on the north side of town.

After that, Nina visited his grave on his birthday, on holidays, and on the Day of the Dead. She did so conscientiously, indulged in self-reproach over his tombstone, and tried to keep horror from overwhelming her as she imagined him beneath her with the desert in his mouth. She stopped paying homage to her guilt and grief on the day she realized Antony was no longer lying in wait for her.

"Aren't you going to the cemetery to visit Tony?" Juanita asked Nina on his birthday. He would have been twenty years old.

"What for?" Nina replied casually. "He's not there. He never was."

Juanita was puzzled but dropped the matter. She did look very carefully at her sister's face to make sure she was not in some kind of trance. As a gesture of good will toward Nina's interest, Juanita had begun attending classes in mind control. It was her way of seeing to it that Nina did not ascend into heaven without her.

Nina and Juanita had loved each other deeply from the beginning. Their passage through the illness and death of their older sister, their suffering from their father's arbitrary nature, their constant sharing even after their marriages and the setting up of separate lives in separate households had bound them irrevocably. If they were unable to see each other during the day, they would speak on the phone as if they had been apart for years. Nina was the pragmatic one for all her later spiritual adventures; Juanita was the idealist and romantic. Nina's poetic nature expressed itself in the subtle mixture of spices with which she served up whatever had been plain meat or poultry.

"My God, Nina, this is delicious. What is it?" Miguel

Chico asked her, tasting a dish that satisfied all but his sense of hearing.

"Roast chicken. Eat it before it gets cold."

After their father's death, Nina and Juanita were left alone in the small house on the south side of town six blocks from the border. Nina cooked all the meals for them and the occasional relatives and friends who stopped by. Juanita cleaned house and did the laundry. Both already had part-time jobs which they kept, but only Juanita finished high school. Nina thought school a waste of time for industrious people with common sense. Unless they had some practical value, books bored her, and she could not bring herself to read novels or stories because daily life and real people were infinitely more interesting to her. Juanita, who joined a book club shortly after she married, could never get Nina to read the latest best seller that arrived monthly and which she read immediately. After thumbing through a few of them, Nina judged them boring and "pure trash." Stories about the endless suffering of southern belles left her unmoved.

"Why don't they write about us?" Nina asked her sister.

"Who wants to read about Mexicans? We're not glamorous enough. We just live," Juanita answered. She was getting ready to go out to the annual policemen's ball with Miguel Grande. Four-year-old Miguel Chico watched his mother show off her new dress. He and the two women were reflected in the mirror of her dressing table.

"Not glamorous enough, huh?" Nina said. "Look at yourself."

Juanita did and saw a tall, slender woman with a long, pale face and dark hair. She was wearing a burgundy-colored dress with a pleated skirt in the style of the early forties, and she delighted her son by turning gracefully from one end of the room to the other so that her dress ballooned out and displayed her beautiful legs. "My mother has glamour legs," he liked to tell the neighborhood.

"The new book came this week," she said to Nina. "Read it after Mickie goes to sleep."

"No thanks. I've got better things to do."

"You're going to remain an illiterate Mexican all your life," Juanita told her as she kissed her son good-night.

"I can read what I need to know. Anyway, in this country, all you really need to know is how to count."

Their aunt Antoinette came up from Mexico City to be with them after their father's death. She was too delicate and ladylike for Nina, but Juanita was delighted with her wardrobe and the few jewels she had brought with her. Antoinette was in her mid-forties and had not married. Mysteriously, she hinted that she had more jewels at home and left the source to Juanita's fancy. Her niece begged her to tell them about the dances and young men of the capital, and the aunt, flattered by the attention, made up stories that satisfied at least one of her brother's daughters. Nina saw through her aunt's pretensions but, so as not to spoil Juanita's pleasure, did not share her insights. After a few months Antoinette was convinced that the girls were safe and could take care of themselves, and she returned to the capital where she lived in a poor section of town, far removed from the fancy dress balls and the pretty young men now part of Juanita's imagination.

Their aunts on their mother's side had families of their own to care for and called infrequently. Nina and Juanita enjoyed their independence immensely. Now they could attend the Saturday night social events sponsored by the Church without having to sneak away and then suffer from the punishments of discovery when they returned home.

"Devil's daughters!" their father had bellowed at them when he found out that they had been to a social and not a religious function. "You are lost!" He, like others from the provinces, was unable to separate the body from the soul.

Their father could be vicious in his rage and was capable of beating them severely when he drank too much. Though she could bear it for herself when he hit them, Nina could not stand to see him hurt her sister. Once she attempted to strike him as he was taking the strap to Juanita. He was so shocked by Nina's temerity that he stopped in the middle of the whipping and walked out of the room without a word. Stunned, the girls could only look at each other in disbelief.

Nina trembled for the rest of the day, waiting in dread to suffer from the consequences of her boldness. The punishment did not come. At the table they sat in their customary silence, a silence broken only by the sounds of their father's eating. They were not permitted to begin their meal until he finished his. As the days went by without his saying or doing anything to her, Nina understood that her punishment was the constant fear of reprisal under which she lived. He was a clever man, she granted him that. But she was his daughter, and her strategy, once she understood, was to pretend to be afraid. Now they sneaked away at will, and their father never touched them again.

On his deathbed, he called for them both and looked at them sadly. Juanita was crying and Nina wondered why. She was glad to be rid of him at last, a sentiment for which she would feel residual guilt until she came upon the spirit world.

"Crybaby, Juanita. What's the matter with you? Remember how he treated us?" To think of him already in the past tense relieved Nina and she refused to give him the satisfaction of her tears. She looked back at him with a straight, impassive face.

"Daughters," he said. "Behave yourselves." He reached for their hands, recoiled from the contact, and died with his mouth and eyes open.

Nina wanted to burst out laughing, but she restrained herself. "Behave yourselves!" It struck her as ridiculous that a man's last words to his children should be so stupid. She hazarded a comment to Juanita as they were being led out of the room by their aunts. "What else have we ever done?"

"Shut up," Juanita said, "have respect for the dead." She had stopped crying at least. With their aunts' permission, they agreed not to tell Tonia that their father was dead. Antonia had stopped asking for him after the time he had visited her in the sanatorium crazy drunk and cursing her for having abandoned him.

Years later, when they told her that Antony was dead, Nina was standing in her kitchen looking out the window at the desert that came right to their back door. Tony had not wanted to move to this house so far away from his friends and favorite cousins. It meant a change in schools for him, and he did not like the idea of having to adjust to new teachers (he had the reputation of being a gifted but "difficult" student), or of leaving his girlfriend behind.

"Now I'll be more isolated than ever," Tony said to his mother. "Is that what you want?" He was sixteen, handsome like his father with Gallic features from Nina's side of the family. His Mexican schoolfriends called him "Frenchie" and teased him for being so good-looking.

"You'll get used to it. And you'll make new friends," Nina said, unwilling to be swayed from her determination to buy the house. "The money we save will put you through college." Tony, like his father, was interested in electrical engineering.

"I don't want to go to college, and your whole life revolves around money."

"Listen to you. If it weren't for the fact that your father and I have worked all our lives to see that you and your sisters live decently, you wouldn't have that car you run around in so much." Nina had been against his having a car at so young an age.

"I bought that car on my own, so don't start in on how grateful I'm supposed to be to you for supporting me. I didn't ask to be born." He was a sophomore in high school.

"If you keep talking to me like that, I'll have your father take that car away from you whether you bought it or not. And you'll go to college because you've got the chance to make something of yourself. Do you hear me, Tony?"

"You never finished high school and you did all right," he said to her.

"It's different now. Besides, I still have to work hard to make ends meet. So does your father."

"It's different now, all right. Everybody's going to college so that they can make more money, and for what? The country's so fucked up, it'll send me to Vietnam before I can even get into college."

"Don't you use bad language in front of me." Nina was not prudish, but she did not like her children to speak that way in her presence. She saw it as an indication of their disrespect for authority and she wondered what her children were learning in school.

"If you make me change schools, I won't study."

"Don't threaten me. You'll change schools if you have to, and you'll study if I have to lock you in your room and throw away the keys to it and your car."

Tony walked away from her.

"Where are you going?"

"Out."

"That's no answer."

"That's the only answer I'm going to give you."

Nina went ahead with the deal for the new house. It was an extraordinarily good buy. In a few years, they could sell it for ten times as much and move back to the part of town they liked best. The money they gained would help put Tony through college. They owned a lot next to the house they were in, and Ernesto was a good engineer. He had built all the homes they had owned. He was as taken by the bargain as she and agreed with her readily over Tony's protests.

The house was one of those new, prefabricated structures that were going up everywhere on the northern and eastern ends of the town. If the economy continued as it had for the last five years, the house would be practically in the middle of town in the next five. At the time they bought it, however, its rear windows looked eastward onto miles of sand and tumbleweed.

Their move was hard on Juanita, who was afraid to drive that far on the highway even in the daytime. "Are you crazy, Nina? You're going to be shoveling sand out of your bathtub."

"What do I care? As long as it doesn't get into my beans, let it do whatever it wants." They moved in during the last days of August. The children changed schools, and Tony fulfilled his threats to stop studying. Nina threatened him in turn with whatever she thought might get him to stop being so obstinate. Juanita was disturbed by their struggle and she tried to interfere once again.

"You're being as stubborn as he is, Nina. Let him have his car so that he can at least get out of the house once in awhile. Tony's young and healthy. You'll make him sick if you continue to coop him up out here in the middle of nowhere."

"I'll let his father give him the keys to the car when he decides to start doing his homework again."

Juanita saw that it was hopeless to argue with her sister about it. She saw obstinacy and grudge bearing as the main flaws in Nina's character, and she was trying to keep them from doing too much damage. She went up to Tony's room.

"Tony, it's your tia Juanita. May I come in?"

"Sure," he said and giggled. "You have to unlock the door from your side. She put in a deadbolt the other day."

Juanita went into his room. Tony was in bed listening to the radio and smoking a forbidden cigarette. His sister, in league with him against their mother, had smuggled it into his room.

"Tony, I know it's none of my business," Juanita began.

"If you're going to try to talk me into doing what she wants, you're wasting your time," he said very quietly.

Instead, she talked to him about her youngest son Raphael, Tony's favorite cousin, and how much they all missed his visits to their house across town. Juanita saw the same faults in her nephew as in her sister and decided that her only course was to pray for them both and hope for the best. But when she went downstairs she said firmly to Nina, "You'd better think very carefully about what you're doing to that boy."

"I have. It's for his own good," Nina said.

The following Easter Sunday they came to tell her that he was dead, drowned at the smelter lake with all his clothes on. She had allowed Ernesto to give Tony the keys to his car for the holiday. As he had walked out the door, she had told him to behave himself.

Nina thought of her father in that moment before she

began howling. "Damn you, Father," she said, inhaling the words, "why do you keep punishing me?" Juanita was holding her tightly from behind, and the two of them rocked together in a slow, horrible dance. She let her go when Nina said she wanted to sit down. Nina walked out of the kitchen, chile still toasting on the burner, and made her way into the living room. Her daughters and husband's relatives were there. She stared at them blindly, sat on the sofa, and resumed her weeping. Her sister-in-law Carmela, Tony's godmother, sat next to her but did not touch her.

In the kitchen, Juanita turned off the burners and, glancing out the window, saw Ernesto standing on the sand, his back to the house. The spring light was still in the sky; the evening would be lovely. Behind her, she heard Miguel Grande say, "Don't go out there. Leave him alone," but she was already out the door and halfway to where Ernesto stood. Looking at the side of his face, for he did not turn to greet her, she sensed that his expression was as dry as the earth beneath them. It chilled her, and all of her instincts could not bear the silence. Quietly, she said to him, "And you, Ernesto? Why don't you cry too?"

He turned to look at her and she thought he was going to strike her. At that moment, he was the loneliest creature she had ever seen. He took her hand and slowly, guided by her, began to feel his loss.

"My son," he said. The desert was in his eyes.

Tony appeared in the sand before him as he had looked on the floor of the emergency room. The medics had taken off all but his trousers, and Ernesto tried to revive him without knowing that the firemen had pronounced him dead by the lake an hour earlier. Miguel Grande and the doctors had to use force to get him away from his son. Police and newspaper photographers were taking flash photos.

Juanita showed one of them to Miguel Chico the following Christmas when he was home for the holidays. As he looked at the photograph, Miguel Chico was struck by his cousin's youth, his athletic chest, the handsome face.

"I don't remember him as grown up as this," he said.

"You didn't bother to see him," his mother answered.

"Don't start, Mother. He didn't exactly care that much for me, you know. He told Raphael that he thought I was a phony."

"That's not true. He loved you."

"It's too late, Ernesto. He's gone," Miguel Grande had told him when he had calmed down somewhat. After the identification forms were signed, he and Miguel Grande walked out of the hospital into the late mid-April afternoon. The day was sunny and warm.

Miguel had parked his police vehicle next to Tony's car. Ernesto noticed it. "Get that car out of my sight," he said angrily to his brother-in-law. "I don't care what you do with it."

They got into the police car. Raphael was waiting in the back seat, having refused to go into the emergency room. None of them said anything during the drive to the house on the east side. Miguel stopped once at a precinct station to phone Juanita and give her instructions. When they arrived, Juanita, Lola, and some of Ernesto's relatives were waiting in their cars. Together they walked to the front door of Nina's house. It was open, the screen door unlatched; the aroma of roasting chiles caused Ernesto to stop dead. He looked at Miguel and Juanita and then walked around the side of the house by himself.

"God damn it," Miguel Grande said for Juanita and Lola to hear, "I'm going to have to tell her." The women followed him into the house.

Ernesto was in the backyard looking at the desert. Seeing it at its most beautiful in the sunset of the holy day, he felt its desolation for the first time in his life. He thought he had always loved it, but now he understood that he had accepted it as a given fact, like breathing. From this day, he could no longer take anything for granted, though his duty as a man was to pretend to do so until the day he died. The vision was overwhelming, and bitterness and despair wrestled with his soul. Both were as dry and timeless as what he was gazing at; only his uncertainty was mortal.

"Why did you swim with all your clothes on? How many times, Antony, have I told you not to go in deep water unless there is someone on the shore?"

After awhile, an angel stood beside him. It asked him in a familiar voice why he did not weep. He thought it a strange question from a creature he had been taught had no emotions. He would ask Nina about it; she would be able to explain it to him. He turned to look at the angel. When he took its hand, it vanished and he saw his sister-in-law Juanita.

The two of them sat side by side on the sand like children, knees drawn up to their chests until the first stars appeared. They astonished him. He was seeing them as if for the first time. A few moments later, he and Juanita got up and went into the house through the kitchen. Ernesto began to weep when he saw the chiles on the stove. Their smell filled the house and he went from room to room opening all the windows.

COMPADRES
AND
COMADRES

On their twenty-fifth wedding anniversary, which Juanita insisted on celebrating in the company of the entire family with a repetition of the wedding vows at the cathedral, Miguel Grande was already in love with her best friend Lola. The late August day was hot, the kind of dry heat that oppresses but does not stifle human activity, and Juanita asked the musicians to set themselves up on the patio of the dream house she and Miguel Grande had at last been able to afford. The affair was to last several years before her husband found the courage to tell her. Until that moment, Juanita did not and would not believe anyone else.

On the day of the celebration, only Miguel Grande and Lola knew about it and Juanita was able to live out and share her fantasy of a stable, if not perfect, marriage that had lasted for a quarter of a century. All of the family was present: Mama Chona, in grey rather than black; the compadres and comadres, the close family friends, Mexican and Anglo, their children and grandchildren. As many people attended this gathering as had attended their wedding in the smaller church on the south side of town closer to the border.

Miguel Grande, a zombie out of duty and habit when forced to be a part of family occasions like this, walked through the ceremony and collaborated in his wife's view of their marriage. Having balked at every preparatory moment, he, not Juanita, looked like the skittish bride at the altar when they repeated the wedding vows. No one present guessed at the truth of his behavior in those weeks before the party. Everyone, especially his own brothers and sisters, knew that he was antisocial and that Juanita was the force who kept him in touch with them. They knew they could rely on him in times of trouble, but they also knew that for reasons of his own, he preferred more and more to maintain a life apart from the family.

Juanita got what she wanted that day and it was to be the last time for many years. After the church service, family and friends were invited to the new house for a dinner dance in the early evening. Juanita wore a pale blue silk dress and her prematurely and completely grey hair gleamed in the rays of light that slanted through the mimosa trees onto the patio. Miguel Grande was wearing the dark blue suit she insisted he buy for the occasion because he had refused to rent the white dinner jacket she thought more appropriate. The first bottle of champagne was opened. It was pink and sweet and purchased by the case more cheaply across the river. Felix gave the toast, paying tribute to the splendid pair whose marriage, he said, was an example to them all, particularly to the younger generation. After applause and a few hoots, Felix—overcome by emotion both feigned and genuine, for he knew his brother well and was at the same time a great sentimentalist—dropped the bottle, recovered it, then served the happy couple their glassful as Juanita handed her small bouquet of garnet red roses to Lola. Lola's tawny hair seemed even brighter because of the dark green chiffon dress she was wearing. She was standing behind Juanita a little to one side so that Miguel Grande could see them both as he drank his wine. The anniversary waltz began to play and Miguel Chico's mother and father danced together while the rest, struck with delight, looked on just as the older generation among them, weeping with emotion, had watched the couple dance twenty-five years earlier, for the greatest sentimental moment in Mexican culture is the coming together of a man and woman in holy matrimony. The waltz ended.

Juanita insisted that Miguel Grande dance with Lola next. El Compa, her husband, had died earlier that summer and Juanita was feeling great sympathy for her. Miguel Chico watched the three of them from the other side of the patio. The sun was behind the foothills and had turned the mountain behind them into a rose-colored stone garden. The trees and shrubs his father had planted in the back and side yards were beginning to freshen the air with their scent, and the crickets, lizards, and sparrows could be heard above the blaring of the mariachi trumpets. Twilight was an hour away.

Miguel Chico watched his mother place his father's hand in Lola's. She kissed them both and went to see about the serving of the dinner. Miguel Chico also noticed that Lola looked at his father as if he were a stranger before he took her in his arms for the next dance. Standing beside Miguel Chico, his eyes snapping into focus through the many cups of wine he had already drunk, his uncle Felix nudged him and said, "Will you look at that?" In another part of the patio, Nina put down her glass, walked toward them, and said to Felix, "Why don't you cut in? They've danced long enough."

Juanita came out of the house. The desert was now the color and texture of her dress and candles were being placed all over the patio and garden according to her instructions. She was very happy and before Felix could reach Lola and Miguel Grande, Juanita intercepted and began dancing with him. Miguel Chico looked at them and at his godmother. Her jaw was locked into place.

"What's wrong, Nina?"

"Never mind," she said quietly, and then, as if on guard against the inevitable, she added harshly, "Nothing. Why don't you go ask Lola to dance with you?" Instinctively Miguel Chico obeyed, and making his way through the dancers toward his father and Lola he saw them with the eyes of his uncle and godmother. His certainty was fixed when he heard the tone of voice in which Lola called his father a *sinverguenza* as he relinquished her to his son. The word is untranslatable; literally, it means "without shame" and can be used as a noun. It was one of Miguel Chico's favorite expressions from childhood. Lola said it darkly, the way lovers would in an embrace. Twirling her about he saw his mother's romantic dreams for herself vanish into the desert evening.

The affair began when El Compa was fixing the roof of his house on a Sunday afternoon in early June. The heat was so unbearable that even the sparrows stopped their racket. As his hands reached for the pain in his chest, El Compa heard only the buzzing of a lone cicada sending out its love signal in the distance toward the poor people's cemetery.

He had decided to make the repairs that day in spite of the heat. His back was better, and he did not want to hear Lola tell him again (as she had every weekend for the past year) that her kitchen would soon be buried under the desert sands if he did not do something about that hole.

"But it's only a little hole, Lolita," he had said to her from the beginning.

"There shouldn't be any holes in this house. God knows we paid enough for it."

She was right. They had paid too much for it, but it was in a good neighborhood, more and more lower class Mexican people like them were moving into it, and everyone knew everyone else just like in the old barrio. Had they waited another six months they would have gotten a better deal, but El Compa wanted to show off and be the first to buy a three bedroom, two bathroom house on that street. He was in his early fifties, and though he had been born on the north side of the river and had taken his stepfather's Anglo surname, El Compa still thought of himself as Mexican. This house was a symbol of his success.

"America is the best goddamned country there is, and don't you forget it," he said to Miguel Chico. They were not related, but El Compa had been in school with his parents and was their closest and most beloved friend.

"You sound just like my father," Miguel Chico said. They were sitting in the den of the newly purchased house watching the news on television. A few months later, the first Catholic president in the history of the country would be assassinated. From the kitchen, Lola informed them that she had just discovered a hole in the ceiling. The men laughed.

"Don't worry, honey. I'll fix it," El Compa said.

"You'd better," she answered. "I'm not about to clean this kitchen every day."

El Compa made a silly face at Miguel Chico. He loved it when women exaggerated; he saw it as their finest weakness. The two of them were still laughing when Lola came into the room, tv dinners in hand.

"Go ahead and laugh, idiots. You'll stop when you find dirt in your food."

"Dirt's not going to get into frozen dinners, sweetheart." El Compa smiled warmly in her direction. Lola turned to Miguel Chico and gave him a dirty look. He stopped laughing and saw why El Compa's son by his first wife did not like Lola and visited only on special occasions. "You know I can't stand for my hands to smell like food. And I'm no servant. I won't live on my hands and knees mopping up dirty floors because you're too lazy to patch up that hole. Pretty soon, we'll have birds flying in and out of the house. Is that what you want?"

El Compa laughed with delight at everything she said, hugged her closely, and winked at Miguel Chico over her shoulder. He loved to spoil her and, after her long fidelity to him, felt it her right to have things the way she wanted them. She made love to him better than any woman he had known, so he did not mind her unhousewifely ways. She was woman where it mattered and refused to become like every other married woman she knew. How many times had he heard that tirade? It did not matter.

El Compa and Lola had met in their teens. He paid her no attention then because he was in love with Sara Cruz and wanted to marry her. Even then, however, all his buddies teased him about being a ladies' man, and several of them, with sly looks on their faces, mentioned Lola's crush on him. She was their favorite, and anyone who could get her attention was on his way to manhood.

El Compa did not care to prove his manhood with her. Sara would be his wife and the mother of his children. It did not even occur to him to take advantage of Lola's beauty in those years. Without being prudish about it, he felt a certain pride in his indifference toward the cool and confident manner in which Lola made them all aware of her creamy breasts and legs. Among the girls, only Sara and her best friend Juanita del Valle did not criticize or label Lola a bad woman.

"What wonderful skin she has," Sara said.

"And that smile," Juanita answered without envy. They admired Lola for being as gorgeous as the movie stars they worshipped every Saturday afternoon at the Colon or Plaza theaters.

El Compa married Sara when he was nineteen. She was a year younger. Two years later—three months after he had started his job on the police force—she bore him a son. His partner and friend, Miguel Angel, married Juanita, and the four of them had good times together. He and Miguel were making steady money and building good reputations for themselves as the first Mexican officers on the force. In Spain, home of some of their ancestors, a civil war was going on. They barely noticed. They were Americans now, even if privately and among themselves they still called each other *chicanitos*. Their great, great grandfathers had long since left Castile to conquer and mix their blood with the natives of Mexico, and death in Madrid meant nothing to them.

On weekends the four of them went to nightclubs across the border, danced all night, and acted like the rich gringos who lived on the hill. At the end of every month the money they spent so lavishly was gone, and they were content to go to each others' houses and play casino after the evening supper of beans and tortillas.

Life was good for El Compa, everything was as he had planned and expected. Both he and Miguel, whose first child was also a boy, gained weight and grew moustaches. At the end of those five years, Sara died of spinal meningitis.

It struck her down without warning, and El Compa felt that his own life had ended. Sara was in the hospital for only a week and Juanita was with her when she died. She phoned the station to inform them. Miguel and El Compa were in the police car when the call came through. They drove to the hospital. In shock, El Compa did not hear the siren Miguel turned on immediately after the call.

"Did she say anything?" El Compa asked Juanita.

"No."

"Did she wake up?"

"Yes, but she just looked at me, Compa. All I could do was cry like a big baby and tell her that everything was all right. What are we going to do without her? Oh, Compa, I'm so sorry."

She put her arms around him and held him like a brother. El Compa loved his comadre Juanita and often chided Miguel for taking advantage of her naivete. He, unlike his compadre, did not sleep with any woman who gave him the chance. Sara and Juanita knew their men and trusted them anyway. When Sara died, they lost a necessary balance.

Lola, who had remained in the background during these years, had also borne a child. She married its father in order to give her son a name but divorced him a year later. Only Juanita had met him. She was able to keep up with Lola after Sara's death because they were both working part-time in the same office downtown. Juanita sensed immediately that Lola's passion for El Compa was not spent, that instead it had grown during the time of his greatest happiness with Sara. Later, Lola confided in Juanita that she had imagined El Compa in all her lovers and pretended that her son was his. She had named him after El Compa.

"Do you mean that he slept with you?" Juanita asked,

at once shocked and fascinated.

"No, comadre. It means that I wish he had."

Juanita did not reply. Lola's beauty captivated her. She was one of those rare Mexican women with green eyes and dark blonde hair. Her light olive complexion was lovelier than ever, and into her fifties her figure would remain taut and fine. Lola moved with a grace that others found irresistible, even if they did not like her. Before her, Juanita felt in the presence of a mystery, awesome and worthy of respect. She accepted Lola as her friend and, after Sara's death, began to confide in her about everything. Lola reciprocated, though she kept some things about her life to herself. Nina and Miguel Grande watched them carefully for different reasons.

Juanita had many friends, for her unselfconscious charity extended to all. Lola had only one friend, and it amazed her how much she could love another woman. Usually, given the choice, she preferred the company of men, but Lola saw in Juanita an innocence she had never possessed. Lola did not covet it, but she stroked and fed it faithfully.

For the first twenty-five years of their marriage, Miguel Grande was content with Juanita's lack of worldly wisdom and the ease with which he could sleep with other women. His only self-imposed rule was not to spend the entire night with them, but to return home to his wife and his sons feeling refreshed and independent.

After they buried Sara, El Compa went to Mexico City by himself. He left his son Frank Jr. with Sara's mother and spent his two-week vacation wandering from hotel to hotel and drinking too much. Every night he went to the Plaza Garibaldi, bottle in hand, and made his way through the crowds of musicians and lovers who sang their praises to

61

mythical heroes or their laments for lost loves. When the glare of the lights became too much for him, he went into El Tenampa and drank until dawn, listening to the mariachis and weeping quietly to himself, disturbed by no one. Once, an ugly woman approached him. She was a part-time cook there who left something for him to eat on the counter after watching him go through the same ritual seven nights in a row. The music of the mariachis, which he ordinarily disliked because of its self-pity, now gripped him and would not let go. Through it, he regained his spontaneous feelings for life and began to laugh without bitterness once again.

He returned to the desert, left his son with Sara's mother, who loved him as her own and brought him up properly, and lived by himself in an apartment not far from where he and Sara had been happy. Gradually, he became absorbed in his job, slept with casual women now and then, visited his son often, and marked time. Sara came to him in dreams and invited him to dance or make love. "My beautiful Compa," she said to him in a dream voice, and he awakened startled and feeling that she was alive. He never asked himself why she had died, but when he interrogated a suspect he sometimes found himself acting from a rage that elated and terrified him. Fifteen years passed. He married a young girl, divorced her two years later, and called up Lola one night to invite her for a drink.

"Juanita, what shall I do?"

"Go with him. It's only for a drink."

"But why? After all these years. His marriage to that little idiot was the limit. What does he want with me now?"

"Don't go then." It was difficult for Juanita to say this, for she was a romantic and wanted El Compa and Lola to be together. Vicarious pleasure in unrequited love was Juanita's weakness. She liked the soap operas on television.

Lola went, showed El Compa what he had been missing, and married him three months later. For Juanita, it was as if the past had returned, only better because now they had more time and money to enjoy themselves. They were together every weekend, and Juanita's other friends were becoming jealous of her time with El Compa and her new comadre.

When Miguel Chico, home from the university for the first time since their marriage, walked into the kitchen on Sunday nights, his parents, El Compa, and Lola sat arguing and laughing over the cards.

"Hello, sweetheart," El Compa said to him. "Where have you been? We've missed you. Come over here and sit down next to your old Compa. Bring me some luck. These *sinverguenzas* are beating my ass."

Miguel Chico sat next to him without feeling restless or uncomfortable, joined in their fun without hesitation, and took sides against Miguel Grande. Juanita liked to see her son laugh. He was becoming much too serious at the university and she did not know what to do about it. The long estrangement between him and his father, for which she felt partially responsible, continued to disturb her. She watched El Compa embrace her son every time he and Lola won a hand. When he was especially elated, he kissed Miguel Chico with great affection, telling him how proud they were of his accomplishments in that big deal college so far away. Juanita noticed that Miguel Chico allowed El Compa to express his feelings without embarrassment, and this pleased her.

"Come on, fairy, let's go home," Lola said to El Compa. His expansive spirit was known and accepted by all with pleasure, but Lola enjoyed teasing him about his affection for other men. As they left, Lola embraced Juanita and Miguel Grande. She kissed Miguel Chico on the mouth. It annoyed him when she forced her tongue between his teeth.

Lola's and El Compa's three years together ended when El Compa died of a heart attack trying to keep the desert out of her kitchen. After the funeral, Juanita went into her own kitchen, opened the cabinets, and threw out all of her old dishes. She replaced them with the elegant white china she had purchased for herself as an anniversary gift. "What am I waiting for?" she said to Miguel Grande. "Life is too short. Why am I saving the luxuries for later? It is later."

Miguel Grande did not hear her. He walked past her to the bedroom, El Compa's badge in his pocket. He tried to take a nap but failed because he could not get Lola out of his mind.

It began at the rosary for El Compa when he saw her in a black dress that showed off her figure. Her eyes were shining without tears. "The black widow," he thought to himself and grinned. Lola caught his eye in that moment, then turned in the direction of the casket. Miguel's stomach began gnawing on his heart.

Lola hated death and everything connected with it. Her instinct was to let the dead die. She was sorry and saddened because El Compa was a good man and had not enjoyed his success long enough, but her passion for him had been realized and spent. Mourning him would not equal the time of hurt she had spent waiting for him to love her. They had had three good years. She was sorry for herself that they had ended so abruptly.

Lola could not bear the weeping women around her. Why should she pay homage to the dead? Even Juanita's blubbering made her impatient. El Compa would be laughing at them all with her now, only in a more kindly way, for he was always nicer than she. She resented the role she must play in this room full of prayers for the made-up thing lying in a quilted box. It was too ridiculous. Frank Jr., standing on the other side of the casket with the men, stared accusingly at her. Lola felt nothing toward him and looked at Miguel Grande instead. His slight grin made her want to burst out laughing and she turned quickly toward the casket.

I don't like you this way, Compa. I don't like you this way at all. Who are all these women in black? They hardly ever speak to me. I've never been respectable enough for them. There's your mother and your old mother-in-law with her. They never liked me. I hate their black veils and their dark brown stockings and their age. The hypocrites make me sick. They loved you until you married me, then they weren't so loving. Hard bitches, I don't believe a single tear. And what does that priest care about you? You were nothing to him and he was nothing to you. What is all this droning about? For what? There's that big *joto* Felix. At least the fairy doesn't care what all these people think about him. You liked him too, my Compa, but why is he moving his mouth like an idiot? And that little prig Miguel, what's he doing here? At least he's not praying. His father's after me already, but I wouldn't mind teaching the kid a few things. It might take that sour look off his face. I want to get out of here, Compa. I'm suffocating. All these words over and over are suffocating me. If I grab Juanita's arm real hard, she'll stop crying and pay attention to me.

"What do you want? What's the matter?" Juanita did not like the expression on Lola's face. She was afraid her friend was going to scream.

"Nothing."

After the rosary, Lola, the two Miguels, and Juanita waited for everyone else to leave. Juanita held her breath as El Compa's mother and Mrs. Cruz, Sara's mother, walked toward Lola to express their grief. They were escorted by

Frank Jr. The last time they had talked, El Compa's mother had told Juanita that she would never again speak to "that woman." Juanita knew it was futile to attempt to make peace between them; Lola's pride would not permit it. The old woman, white haired, slim, and elegant, approached them slowly. Sara's mother, on Frank Jr.'s arm, was a few steps behind her. The two women had just finished paying their last respects in front of the casket, and Juanita had watched Mrs. Glass touch her son's face. Juanita was not afraid of Mrs. Cruz, but she gave plenty of room to the woman who had buried two husbands and now her only son. Mrs. Glass's eyes, like her voice, were dry.

"Juanita, how are you?" She spoke in Spanish. "And you, Miguel and Miguelito? How happy I am to see you always, whatever the circumstances. Come and visit me at home next week, will you? I want to talk to you." Juanita mumbled inaudible replies and very carefully directed her toward Lola, who was standing by the door of the mortuary. Mrs. Glass walked in a measured and solemn way, staring hard at Lola, as she passed her by without a word. Sara's mother nodded shyly at her and said very softly in Spanish, "I'm so sorry."

Lola held her back. "I am too, Señora Cruz." Juanita hoped Lola would stop there. "But I am happy to know that today El Compa is with Sara." Mrs. Cruz embraced Lola without looking to Mrs. Glass for permission, and they walked out of the mortuary together. Frank Jr. and Mrs. Glass were waiting for them at the bottom of the stairs. Refusing to respond to the sound of his mother's name on Lola's lips, Frank Jr. noticed how well made-up she was and, to make sure she had no chance to kiss him, quickly took his grandmother's hand and helped her into the car. Lola ignored Mrs. Glass completely.

She knew the effect her words would have on Sara's mother and was pleased to have gotten even with Mrs. Glass for snubbing her. In fact, Lola was not glad that her man was out in the pure serene with his first wife. If they were floating around somewhere, disembodied spirits, she was jealous. Only the thought that they couldn't have sex consoled her.

"What a beautiful thing you said to Mrs. Cruz, Lola. I thought you were going to put your foot in it," Juanita told her as Miguel drove them back to El Compa's house.

"That old fool. What do I care about her? She thinks that one hug can make up for all the insults they've made behind my back all these years."

"She's never said anything about you. You're being unfair."

"Well, it's the same thing. She never came to see me or invited me to her house. Every time I invited her, she refused. Anyway, who cares about those old ladies? They loved taking all that crap from their men so that they could act like martyrs after the men died. I don't like old bags who wear black all the time. El Compa's death is going to give them another excuse to suffer for a plaster god who doesn't give a damn about them or their moaning. Why aren't they dead? My Compa is gone. He was young. What are they doing still alive?"

"They ask themselves the same thing, Lola." Juanita replied quietly, suppressing her opposition even though she did not like Lola's tone or her lack of respect for religion and old people. "Why don't you cry?" she asked before she could stop herself.

"Because I'm not mad enough," Lola answered in a hard tone.

Miguel Chico was shocked. Miguel Grande smiled to

himself as he saw them reflected in the rearview mirror. He asked himself how he could live without them. Together, they made him happy and filled his life.

His passion for Lola began in that way. The look they had exchanged during the rosary planted the seed of longing for her in that place near his groin and heart where he was most vulnerable. He already knew how she made love. Years before he had taken her to bed and had recognized her as an equal there. Once that was settled, he had been content to let it rest, especially after she and Juanita became so close. But now with El Compa gone, something had changed. There was a shift he neither understood nor knew enough to fear, in a direction toward which a soft wind was blowing, scented with her perfume. Years of indulgence in the flesh of beautiful women, like all those years of smoking, did not help him turn away from Lola and her scent. Instead, they helped him sniff her out, discover her most vulnerable place, and show it to her. The revelation ruined the three of them for a time.

Miguel Chico, riding in the front seat with his father, began to feel sick to his stomach. He hated the smell of cigarette smoke, and the summer night made it hang heavy in the car even with the windows open. Lola and his father smoked all the way to her house. The tools El Compa had used still remained on the roof because Lola refused to let anyone touch them. As they walked to the door, Miguel Chico fought his nausea. Finally, he went to the toilet and vomited. Juanita, accustomed to his weak stomach from birth, was not troubled. Lola knocked on the door and offered him a glass of water.

"No, thank you," he said as impersonally as possible. He feared her power and could not stand her touch.

"All right, baby, I'll leave it right here on the table by

the door. It's got ice in it, and it'll help to settle your stomach."
He waited until he heard her walk away before he opened the
door and drank the water in gulps. It gave him cramps and he
sat down on the toilet waiting for them to pass.

"Mickie, let's go," his father shouted from the living
room. He was never sick and he ignored the illnesses of
others.

"I'll be right there," he answered. There was blood in
his stool.

"Are you sure you want to stay alone tonight?" Juanita
asked Lola as they were leaving. "You know you can come
over to our house."

"I'll be all right. I need to be by myself after today,"
she said. Miguel Chico watched as his parents, first his
mother, then his father, hugged her.

After El Compa's death, Lola regularly began calling
Miguel Grande to her house across town to help her with
mechanical chores. He stopped up the cracks in the roof and
the desert shifted from the kitchen into her heart. She was
always thirsty. Her friendship with Juanita did not seem
strong enough to withstand her greater need for the love of
a man, and her conscience, long since discarded, seemed lost
forever.

"Listen, comadre, is Miguel there?"

"Yes, comadre, what do you need?"

"You know, there's always something wrong with
something. This time it's the garden hose. Can you ask him
to come over and fix it?"

"Sure. I'll send him right over."

As she hung up the phone, Lola asked herself what
she thought she was doing, but not in any serious way. Not
until she had fallen in love with him did she feel afraid of
what might happen to all of them.

In the meantime, she enjoyed her moments with him. Their lovemaking, which they arranged easily, left them exhausted but never satiated. On weekends they all spent time together, and Lola often slept in Mickie's room when he was away at school. Juanita's other friends began to warn her, but she remained loyal to Lola.

"Look, comadre, your little friend has no shame. You'd better keep an eye on her. She's after your husband."

"I don't believe it and you'd better stop telling me such things or we won't be friends any more. She's my friend and I trust her." In Juanita's mind, El Compa was still alive and keeping Lola company. To think that her best friend would betray his memory with her husband was beyond the possible to her.

So Lola, Miguel Grande, and Juanita went to parties, movies, and dances together. Miguel began guarding Lola closely when she danced with other men, and after such occasions they fought vehemently.

"I saw the way you were dancing with that queer Pepe."

"Oh? He's a very good dancer. And he's no queer."

"How would you know? All good dancers are queer and you know it." Miguel shared the macho's distrust of any man who was too handsome or danced too well. "Did he spend the night here?"

"Hey, Miguel, that's none of your business." Lola tried to speak in a matter-of-fact tone, but she was getting more and more angry with him and she knew she was lost if she showed her anger.

"Well, you didn't have to kiss his ass all night."

"I don't kiss anybody's ass, Miguel. And I can do anything I want to. We're not married, remember?"

He stared at her with rage. He could not understand

how she could speak to him like that. He wanted to kill her and felt she should be begging him for mercy after all he had given up for her. He did not know why he couldn't bring himself to tell her that the things she did hurt him deeply.

When he forced her to the couch she knew she had won. Men were easy to deal with sexually. Without a word and very quickly she took off her clothes, and he was at her. Her knowledge of these mysteries helped her say several times without meaning it, "Hurt me, Miguel, hurt me." She moaned as if indeed he were and, in that way, gave him the illusion that he was in control once again.

Nina was aware of their games after she saw them dance at the twenty-fifth wedding anniversary party. At the weekly poker games, she observed carefully the ways in which Miguel Grande was attentive to Lola. At first she attributed it to his concern for her well-being after El Compa's passing. After the anniversary celebration, she knew better.

It was the way Miguel lit Lola's cigarette that confirmed Nina's suspicions. He made a point of the gesture, causing an infinitesimal lull in the game as he stopped to attend to Lola's needs. And he did it with a grace Nina had never noticed in him, certainly a grace he did not extend to her sister whose wants he saw to with care, but casually or with constant complaining. The motion of his arm, lighter in hand, and the way Lola drew the flame toward her face, her own fingers resting in a silky way on his, the instantaneous meeting of their eyes and the just-as-instantaneous return to the cards as Miguel clicked the flame out without blowing on it as he usually did. The entire ritual fascinated and disgusted Nina.

How dumb do they think I am, she asked herself, and

tested her observations by asking her brother-in-law to light her own cigarette. He did so without ceremony and as always. Nina stopped looking at her cards in order to set firmly in her mind the full implications of his gesture. Such evidence would come in handy when Juanita discovered for herself what was going on. From experience, Nina knew it would take her unworldly sister a long, long time, for she trusted everyone and everything.

"What are you doing with those cards, stupid?" Lola asked Miguel, and everyone at the table laughed. She alone got away with belittling him in front of others without having him retreat into hurt masculine pride. "Deal and get it over with." Nina noted the honey in her voice.

As he dealt, Miguel commented on every card, a habit of his that drove Nina to distraction. "A trey, a deuce, a queena, a *joto*, a five-a, an eighter from Decatur, and an ace for me." Only it wasn't, it was just a four. Nina was glad. The queen was hers and she bet three cents on it knowing that Miguel would raise it to a nickel. "Un neekle," he said, too impatient to wait for the others to throw their money into the pot.

"All right, the boat's loaded. Pair of treys for Juanita."

"Ay, how good," Juanita said. She was sitting on his left and Lola was on the other side of him.

"A ten for sourpuss." Nina's husband, out a dime, picked up his cards and slammed them down in real disgust, wondering out loud why he had such terrible luck and vowing to quit playing poker altogether.

"Oh, Ernesto, don't be such a spoilsport," Lola said, but she failed to seduce him back into the game. Nina watched her carefully from across the table.

"Pair of queenas for the Nina."

"Tenk joo berry mahch," she said in a hammed up Mexican accent.

"There's a six for your *joto*, Memo."

"Thanks," the lifelong poker friend answered, "let's see if they can make it together."

His wife Carla snickered. She drank too much and took a long time figuring out what cards she held. She won often.

"Possible straight," Miguel said to her.

"And a king for the widow." Lola glared at him warmly and then looked around him at Juanita to make sure they both disapproved of his lack of respect for the dead. She was protecting herself nicely, Nina saw.

"And an ace!" This time it was. "And I bet another nickel."

"I'll bet three cents."

"To a nickel," he said immediately.

"Of course, I knew you'd do that," Nina replied.

"Why don't you raise me? You've got a pair of queens."

"Because you'll raise me after."

"No, I won't."

"Yes, you will."

"No, Ninita, I promise. Trust me," he said in his most charming voice.

"Okay. Three more cents."

"To a nickel!" he upped the bet quickly.

"I knew it, you big liar."

Nina loved these games. Cards excited her, and winning at poker or blackjack was one of her great pleasures. Her thrill came in watching Fortune at work in such tangible ways, and her pulse quickened at the turn of each card as they drew closer to the end of the deal. Her queens held steady; she knew she had some chance in seven card stud, nothing wild. Juanita was still in the game with two threes showing. Lola had a possible high straight. Memo and Carla were out and Miguel just had that one fat ace showing and not much else. He was such a bluffer, she knew he had nothing underneath to back it up.

"Your bet, sweetie-pie," he said to her.

"Wait a minute. I'm thinking."

"You're not here to think. You're here to play poker."

"Oh, leave her alone," Lola and Juanita said at the same time. Nina was unable to concentrate on the cards because she was overwhelmed by the spectacle across the table from her. For the first time, she wanted to break her resolve and warn her sister.

"I check," she said finally.

"Check," said Lola.

"A nickel," Miguel said, and they all threw in their money.

"All right," Nina said, "let's see what all you bluffers have got." She turned up her cards to show that she had a pair of deuces to go with her queens. Lola's pair of kings was not enough.

"Aces and sixes," Miguel said, reaching out for the pot and scraping it toward him. "Come to papa."

"Wait a minute," Juanita said. "I have three treys." Nina was delighted. She was always glad to see her cocky brother-in-law defeated.

"That's my herman," she said to her *hermana*. They had Anglicized the word for sister and used it as a term of endearment with each other. "Deal me out," she told Juanita as she got up from the table. "I'm going to get something to eat. Anybody want some enchiladas? They're from yesterday, but they're delicious."

A few minutes later, Lola joined her in the kitchen. Nina was not able to look her in the eye as Lola went on about the new clothes she had bought for her trip to Los Angeles. She was going to visit her son, who had moved there years earlier. Nina listened to the tone of Lola's voice and decided that her suspicions were well founded. She wondered how much money Miguel was giving her.

Miguel Grande had told himself many times that he would be able to extricate himself from his involvement with Lola and treat her as he had in the past, as someone important, but not basic, to his life. Now he felt that without her, his heart would dry up like a scorpion in the sun. There was no one to turn to for counsel, and even if there had been, he would have had difficulty admitting that he found himself increasingly unable to control his emotions. Such an admission of weakness would demean him before those very men who gossiped about his exploits with admiration.

"How's the wife?" they asked. And the more daring added, "How's the widow?"

"Just fine," he replied, a hint of the braggart in his voice to let them know he understood what they were asking.

His sister Eduviges' husband Sancho said to him one day after tuning up his car, "You're really a disgrace, you know that?" Sancho's sympathies were with Juanita, for he knew what it meant to be married for life to a member of the Angel family. Miguel pretended not to understand the remark, but the pointed way in which it had been said made him aware that the family knew about Lola. He dismissed Sancho as envious and less than a man.

Any man worthy of the name, Miguel reasoned, must envy the joy and excitement in his heart when he walked into places with a woman on each arm. On one side, his wife and the mother of his sons. On the other, the woman who brought ecstasy to his everyday life. Sometimes his heart contracted with the anticipation of being found out by

Juanita or rejected by Lola. In those periods, he treated his fellow officers to such extremes of mood that some of them suggested he take a vacation. He said he would after the new chief of police was named.

By seniority he was entitled to the position and he even allowed himself to feel confident about getting it. The force, like the town, was more than half Mexican now, a ratio he had worked hard for over twenty-five years to bring about. The town seemed ready to accept people of Mexican ancestry in positions of power. Indeed, five years earlier a man from their background had been elected mayor, despite smear campaigns and threats of violence against him and the town's Mexican people.

Juanita's oldest aunt, Tia Cale, had even gotten out of her sickbed to vote for the man. In a weak moment, Miguel had agreed to drive her to the polling station if she could get out of the house. Tia Cale had not left either house or bed in all the years he had known her.

"Are you ready?" Juanita had asked him on election day.

"Ready for what?"

"Tia Cale just phoned. She's dressed and waiting for us to pick her up. She's going to vote."

Miguel was annoyed, but he went for her. Tia Cale had lost quite a lot of weight, but she was tall and big boned, and as he and Juanita carried her to the car Miguel calculated that she weighed about a hundred and eighty pounds. She behaved like a young girl on her first date and apologized constantly for the old black hat that kept falling off and for the way her stockings kept sliding down to her ankles.

"Forgive me, forgive me," she said again and again in Spanish, looking at them to show that she understood what a burden she was. Miguel, normally aloof, teased and tickled her until Juanita got so mad she refused to help carry if they were going to behave like children. "Now they can't say that I'm an illiterate Mexican," the old lady said as they put her back to bed and said good-bye.

The man Tia Cale helped elect was an honest, middle-class citizen who had been educated in the public schools they all knew. He served competently and without incident, and his only gesture of rebellion was to apply for member-ship in the town's country club shortly after his election. He was denied official, but given honorary, status in the club. After his three-year tenure as mayor he was appointed am-bassador to a Latin American country, and in his farewell speech he referred to the high standards of the town's most exclusive club with an irony that made even those who had opposed him laugh at themselves. But the restrictions re-mained in effect.

Miguel Grande knew how intransigent the power structure was, but he respected and defended it against Communist ideas like those his son was learning at the uni-versity. He bragged about Miguel Chico's abilities and achievements to others and sentimentally believed that his oldest boy was fulfilling his own dreams of a college educa-tion—dreams he had never in fact had—but he believed that all college professors without exception were Communists. In this view, the rest of the state concurred.

When Miguel went against the interests of his own men, he convinced himself that he did so with an eye toward gaining something for them in the long run. His long run was coming to an end and it coincided with the plans he was making to be with Lola. He and the four other candidates for chief had taken the exam, which was only a formality, and they were waiting to hear who would be chosen. As chief, he could make some changes that needed to be made, and he would draw a salary that would get him out of debt for the first time in his life. He would move Juanita to a smaller house and gradually free himself so that he could spend more time with Lola.

The North American dream had worked for him. Only his family reminded him of his roots, and except for his mother he avoided them as much as possible.

"It's Jesus Maria's birthday," Juanita told him.

"So?" He changed the tv channel with his new remote control gadget.

"I bought a present for you to give her."

"You give it to her."

"You're awful, Miguel. She's your sister."

"She's never given me anything except lectures about going to church. I'm not going to her house. Go by yourself."

Juanita visited his sisters with a regularity that at first pleased Jesus Maria and Eduviges and then irritated them because they were unable to lie about their ages in her presence without causing an argument. As Juanita grew older, they grew younger. The sisters respected Miguel for the esteem he brought to the family name, but they did not approve of him. They wanted him to be chief of police, but they also wanted him to get rid of Lola. "It's a scandal," Jesus Maria said to Eduviges. She did not, however, say it to Miguel Grande, even though she was his older sister.

After Juanita left, Miguel Grande stared at the police adventure story unwinding on the screen. Next year he would see it in color. He lit another cigarette and wondered what to do with his women. If his brother Armando were alive he could ask him for advice. Miguel Grande had never forgiven his brother for moving to Los Angeles without him.

Armando had been like a father to him and he knew about women. His green eyes, so like Lola's, had attracted them like bees to honey. Miguel needed someone's counsel, for the love he felt toward both women was wearing him down.

And so his heart, alternately swelling and shriveling, began to humble him. He thought of visiting Miguel Chico in San Francisco and confessing to him. Perhaps his son could say the words that would show him the way out of this tangle. He found himself having to be more careful in ways that made him look back wistfully to less complicated days when he wandered at will among secretaries and waitresses. Lately, he had begun calling one woman by the other's name. Juanita did not notice. Lola, her nose sniffing danger, said, "What's the matter with you? Are you crazy?" The greatest mystery of all was how much he thought of his wife when he was with Lola. And when he was with Juanita, he could only think of his beloved on the other side of town.

"Asshole," he said to himself, "you've screwed yourself."

A few nights later, Miguel Grande had just fallen asleep when the phone began to ring. Juanita, lying on her side with her good ear to the pillow, remained sleeping throughout the conversation. At first, Miguel thought it was the chief, for the voice on the other end was authoritative and the words were spoken in a heavy Texas accent. Slowly, he understood that the call was from the army base on the other side of the mountain, and that it was about his brother.

"Are you Felix Angel's brother?" The man pronounced the last name in English and momentarily confused Miguel.

"Yes, yes, I am. What's the problem?"

"We've got your brother here, and we need someone to identify him."

"What's the matter? What's going on?"

"Just get right on over here, will you?"

Miguel drove to the base in his police car. At that hour there was no need for the siren or the warning lights, but he felt them inside his brain. He drove by Lola's house on the way to see that all was in order. Her car was parked in its usual place and the bedroom window drapes were partially drawn in their customary way. It calmed him to think of her sleeping quietly and he fought the impulse to let himself in, lie down beside her, and hold her. He had told Juanita that he would return as soon as he had checked on this emergency call. She told him to be careful and rolled over to his side of the bed. He left her asleep. Some moments later a premonition nudged her awake. She got up, dressed, and made coffee. When he returned an hour before dawn, Miguel found her sitting in the kitchen waiting for him.

At the base, Miguel was met at the gate by the man who had phoned him and who now escorted him to a waiting room in the infirmary. On the way, he thought he saw Felix's car, but he did not ask about it. Miguel suspected that Felix had been caught playing around with a soldier, had gotten into some kind of a fight, and was now in the next room with a few broken bones and some teeth missing. He hoped there were no newspapermen around because such a story would have some effect on his chances for chief.

"Goddammit, Felix, you've got a wife and four kids. When are you going to learn not to fool around with the little boys?" Miguel was practicing his speech.

When he was allowed into the next room, two of his plainclothesmen were already there waiting. They responded wordlessly to his greeting, then looked at the table in the middle of the room. A man in white lifted the sheet.

It was unrecognizable. There was no face, and what looked like a tooth was sticking out behind the left ear. Dried blood and pieces of gravel stuck to the skin. The eyes were swollen shut, bulbous and insectlike. The back of the head was mushy. The rest of the body was purple, bloated, and caved in at odd places. One of the testicles was missing.

"That's not my brother," Miguel said quietly.

No one replied. His men showed him a wallet containing all of Felix's identification papers and then they handed him a brown paper bag. In it was Felix's favorite sweater covered with dirt and blood. When he touched it, Miguel began to yell.

"Who did this? Who killed my brother?"

His men fought him to the floor and he heard the doctor instruct them to bring him into the office. Miguel stopped struggling and asked them to let him go. The doctor signaled his assent, and Miguel, hugging the brown paper bag, followed them down the corridor. Felix had been found in the back seat of his car during the midnight routine inspection. He seemed to be sleeping, turned on his side, his back to the flashlights. The soldiers on duty had knocked on the windows in an attempt to wake him, but when they saw that his head was bleeding they forced their way into the car. Had he been called an hour earlier, the doctor might have kept him alive for a few days, but Felix would probably not have regained consciousness. There were no signs of a weapon and no clues. It was clear he had been beaten to death. At the moment, they were doing everything possible to find out who had driven the car onto the post.

"Felix, you stupid fool," Miguel muttered.

"Beg your pardon?" the doctor said.

"Nothing."

"I'm very sorry, Captain. We called you because of the

last name. You're well known around town and we took the chance. Your men seemed certain that he was your brother."

Miguel was aware of noting the doctor's Texas accent rather than hearing what he was saying. He felt nauseous.

"Thank you, Doctor." As he left the room, Miguel instructed one of his men to carry on with the investigation and to call him as soon as they found any leads. Then he asked where the men's room was.

He began to cry soundlessly as he sat on the toilet, the tooth behind Felix's ear continuing to glint at him obscenely. In that private place, he felt an odious mixture of rage and grief. In all his years of dealing with humanity at its worst, he had never seen a body so mangled by another human being. "They better not let me near the son of a bitch who did this," he said out loud. He stopped crying, left the stall, and washed his hands and face slowly. He avoided looking in the mirror. Paper bag in hand, he left the base without speaking to anyone else. He drove home past the canyon and along the mountain road. The moon was setting as he walked from the car into the house. The air was dry ice.

"What's the matter? What happened?" Juanita asked, handing him a cup of coffee.

"Don't ask me any questions right now. I don't want any coffee. Put on your coat, it's very cold. We have to go to Felix's house right away. Your comadre Angie is going to need you." Juanita was the only comadre Felix's wife could tolerate.

"But Miguel, tell me what happened. Is Felix all right?"

"Wait, will you? I'll tell you on the way. Get your coat."

He looked defeated, and his face and the tone of his voice kept Juanita from asking any more questions. The paper bag he held terrified her.

On the way Miguel told her everything as if it were a police report and gave her strict instructions not to repeat any of these details to Angie. He would tell her only that Felix was dead and that the causes were under investigation.

"Oh, my God," Juanita said, "who would do a thing like that to him? He was the kindest man I ever knew. Who would hurt him like that?" The facts were too monstrous for her, and she, who cried readily over anything happy or sad, remained dry eyed as she faced them. She was thinking of Angie. "You know Angie is going to want a rosary with an open casket, Miguel. What am I going to tell her?"

"Don't tell her anything. Agree to everything. I'll make whatever arrangements need to be made. Please do as I say for once."

They drove the rest of the way in a silence interrupted only by the police calls on the radio. Miguel listened attentively to each, hoping that his men had uncovered something. Ordinarily everyone, even he, treated the death of a Mexican in a routine, casual manner. This time, because of him, the newspapers would take notice.

"Felix, you never thought about the rest of us," he said aloud. Juanita did not respond.

They had arrived at Felix's house. "Wait here until I get them to open the door. I want to tell Angie and JoEl first. You come as soon as you see me go in, understand?" When she saw the house, Juanita started to cry.

"And stop crying before you come in."

"I can cry if I want to. What do you think I'm made of?" Looking at the paper bag in his hands, she had the eerie illusion that Felix was inside it. When she had earlier offered to take it from his lap, Miguel, clutching it even more tightly, had refused to let her touch it.

For a moment, as he walked toward the house, Miguel

saw Felix as a child dancing in the rain. His throat began to ache and to stifle his thoughts he started pounding on the front door. When, after what seemed a long while, he heard noises from within, the winter light of dawn had reached the front of the house. He shivered, aware of another coldness. Sand from the early dust storm the day before gleamed with frost.

"It's Miguel," he shouted. "Open the door."

Waiting for the grand jury investigating her father's death to reach its decision, Felix's daughter Magdalena sat with Miguel Grande in one of the small cubicles of the federal building downtown. The bar where Felix had picked up the young man who killed him was across the street and around the corner. The sterility of the room made Lena remember the lobby at the morgue where she had waited to see her father's body. The official in charge had not allowed her to see Felix and told her that Miguel Grande had already made a positive identification.

"But you don't understand," she told him, "he was my father."

"I'm sorry, miss. I've got my orders."

Lena had remained seated opposite the official's desk until the assistant had asked her to leave. Except for that occasion, she had not been in such buildings.

When Miguel Grande had told her family about Felix's death, Lena sensed he was hiding something. Later, at the rosary, she was grateful for the custom that had moved her mother to insist upon an open casket. Lena had knelt staring furiously at the body, for the mortician had not been able to disguise the horror her father had endured, and she wept more out of rage than grief.

By then, rumors about the circumstances of his death had reached them. The newspapers had run front page articles about the incident, and she and the others in the family who loved him had filled in the details for themselves. "The family," as usual—more concerned with its pride than with justice—had begun to lie to itself about the truth.

Lena was a scandal to the family because she ran around with the "low class" Mexicans in her high school. She was not a good student like Yerma or her cousin Miguel Chico, whom she judged "goody-goodies." To Lena being young meant having fun and she enjoyed herself in ways that horrified her father's sisters and would have shocked Mama Chona had she known. Lena helped organize a club of Mexican girls called "Las Rucas," and they sponsored dances which the *pachucos* attended faithfully. Lena became very popular with them for she had a good voice and the bands that played for the dances regularly asked her to sing.

In all these activities, Felix defended her strongly against the objections of Jesus Maria, Eduviges, and Miguel Grande. Her uncle, unlike her aunts, was worried about her physical safety and not her virtue. "I'm safer with them than with the gringos," she told him. She did not speak to her aunts, and when family occasions demanded that they be together, Lena put on more makeup than usual and wore the shortest, tightest skirt she could find. Later, her father would make his wife Angie laugh by imitating the looks on his sisters' faces as they tried not to notice Lena's appearance.

The hypocrisy of the family enraged her, and when she began to realize that the sexual implications of her father's murder were going to keep them from strongly pursuing justice, she took matters into her own hands. Angie was the only member of the family Lena respected in those days, but she was unapproachable, refusing to listen to anything that soiled the memory of her husband. On the day of Felix's funeral Lena stopped trying to talk her mother into avenging his death. Throwing the clods of dirt into his grave, Angie paused and said distinctly for all to hear, "Felix, I want you to rest in peace. You've suffered enough." After that, Lena went directly to Miguel Grande.

"Tio, I want to know what happened. And I want you to tell me the truth."

"No you don't."

"Yes, I do, God damn it. And if you don't tell me, I'll find out on my own and cause as much trouble as I can."

She was seventeen and possessed a toughness that Miguel found attractive in women. She was short for her age, her breasts too large, her legs skinny, her complexion too dark, but she moved with Lola's grace. "All right," he said, "I'll tell you, but you're not going to like it, and I don't want you to repeat any of this to your mother."

Lena wept throughout, especially when she remembered her father's gentle nature, but she wept without knowing it, and when she looked at Miguel as he finished his story, she was surprised that her face was wet. "I wish I was a man," she said immediately. "I'd kill that little son of a bitch." Her vehemence astonished Miguel who had thought of her as just another of Felix's spoiled brats, and he was not prepared for the tone of her next question.

"What do you think of all this, Tio?" She asked with a child's wonder that almost broke him.

He resorted to his official line, "I don't care what my brother did. I loved the hell out of him."

When Miguel thought about his brother after all the facts were known, he felt ashamed and frustrated. He had never been able to understand Felix's obsession and did not want to. The thought of touching another man in those ways disgusted him, and his knowledge that Felix enjoyed doing such things had created a barrier between them that neither ever made the effort to overcome.

When they were children Felix enjoyed behaving like a clown, putting on his mother's straw hat, mincing and dancing about in ways that made even Miguel laugh. As they grew older, Felix's behavior embarrassed Miguel Grande, and he hoped that the stigma of being *jotos* would not reach past his brother.

An assistant from the DA's office came to escort them, even though Miguel Grande had been to that office many times. The formality reminded Lena that her uncle had not been allowed near the place where her father's murderer was being kept in custody. The attorney shook hands with Miguel Grande in a broad, friendly manner and nodded politely toward Lena. She sat down facing him as he explained how the evidence convincingly showed that her father was in fact "excuse me, ma'am" a homosexual and that he had seduced other men, some of whom were willing to testify during a jury trial. The attorney thought it useless to subject the family to the shame and embarrassment of such an investigation. The young soldier had acted in "self-defense and understandably," given the circumstances, and there was no reason to prosecute him. He had already been transferred to another base.

Lena knew her opinion meant nothing, for she was a minor. She waited for her uncle to raise the obvious objections, to express the deep rage she felt at such injustice. Miguel Grande remained silent. He was as helpless as she, and in her ignorance she decided that his love for her father was without conviction, and that once again the family pride had led him to humiliate himself before men who did not give a damn about people like them. She was stunned. Had she been permitted to say anything, she told Miguel Chico many years later—after she had moved to California and could talk about it—she would have asked two questions. "What is the name of the son of a bitch who killed my father? I'll kill him myself since you men can't think about anything but your balls." And to the district attorney: "How many times have you sucked a cock, you prissy fool, or gotten some whore to suck yours?"

As Miguel Grande drove her home, Lena looked at him with different eyes and said to no one in particular, "God, what a family." He said nothing but felt some shame which was tempered by the knowledge that when she grew older she would understand and forgive him. In the police car outside her father's house, they talked.

"Will you tell your mother, brother, and sister about the DA's decision?"

"Yes, Uncle."

"Will you try not to think about it any more, Lena, for your father's sake?"

"Yes, Uncle."

"I'm very, very sorry, Lena."

She faced him. "Tell it to the judge, you fucking hypocrite." She slammed the door and ran into the house. A few months later she was glad to find out that he had not been selected chief, thinking it might force him to understand what life was really like for "low class" Mexicans in the land that guaranteed justice under the law for all.

When Miguel Grande told his oldest son that he was in love with his mother's best friend and did not know what to do about it, they were sitting in the study of Miguel Chico's home in San Francisco. For the first time Miguel Chico felt that his father was talking to him as an equal, and that sense, more than the distraught man before him, made him respond with some patience.

The phone calls from the desert had begun earlier in the week, and he had been annoyed that his own schedule had to be adjusted to accommodate the stupidities of his father. He was in the prudish period of his life; the operation that would change everything was a few years away.

"Mickie, I'm coming to see you. Do you think you can spare the time?" His father's voice lacked its usual sarcastic edge, a shift Miguel Chico caught immediately.

"Sure, Dad. When do you think you'll get here?"

"Well, Nina wants to fly up there and meet us. Your mother, Lola, and I will drive up in the middle of the week."

"I'll be here. Just phone when you're within two or three hours of getting into the City."

"All right son. I sure appreciate it."

His father only called him "son" in that tone when he wanted to discuss a serious matter, and Miguel Chico could tell that something was very wrong. He knew that everyone except his mother was aware of the affair between Lola and his father but he didn't understand why his godmother was coming too. He considered the possibilities without worry or involvement. His father's antics had long since stopped affecting him directly except when he was with his family during the holidays. The old childhood feelings were then dredged up and he had to be alone for several days after his return to the West Coast. To recover, to rid himself of the desert, he walked on the beach or in the fog.

His curiosity about his parents was purely intellectual now, and it amused him perversely to see his father caught between the two women in his life. Clearly, he had not yet told Juanita about the affair or she would not be driving out with them. Even his mother's masochistic streak was not that wide—or if it was, she too had been buried by that desert. He spent the week waiting for them. Nina arrived first. He met her at the airport and they were able to talk as she was preparing dinner for the two of them before the others came.

"There's something wrong with your father," she began. "Do you know what's going on?"

"No, I don't, Nina. You see them all the time. If you don't know, who does? When I phone them, he asks me if I'm angry with them and tells me dirty jokes. Mother tells me who has died and who is getting married or having kids."

It pained him to play this cat and mouse game with his godmother. Ordinarily they were able to talk with candor and mutual curiosity, even if they did not agree. Now they were forced into evasive tactics, and disgust for his father began seeping into Miguel Chico's voice; already he felt himself assuming the son's role of blaming the father for the wretchedness of the world.

"Well," Nina said, "he's been acting very strange lately, and it's driving your mother crazy."

Miguel looked at his godmother. Her hair was salt and peppery, her eyes watery in a disturbing way he did not remember. Still, they were as alert as ever, and he now saw the mark of obstinacy in her jaw as an emblem of survival. The last time they had spent time alone together was a year after Antony's death. The slackness of her expression then as he helped her set tile in the bathroom of the house Ernesto had built in the old neighborhood had bothered him. Miguel Chico could not understand why they had moved next door to the house Tony had loved and begged them not to leave, the house where he had lived most of his life. It was, he thought, another sign of the Catholic guilt and desire for punishment that plagued his parents' generation and from which there seemed no escape. In his arrogance, Miguel believed he was finding ways out of it through his university education. He had not yet had time to combine learning with experience, however, and he still felt himself superior to those who had brought him up and loved him.

"What do you mean 'strange'? What is he doing? Does it have anything to do with Felix? That really tore him apart, you know. And when he didn't get chief of the department, he lost a lot of faith in himself and what he's believed in all his life about this country. I'd be acting 'strange' about all that myself, Nina. Anybody would."

"This is different."

"How?" Miguel noticed how carefully Nina was watching his face as she spoke.

"A few months ago he broke out in hives, and when your mother wanted to rub ointment on them he accused her of having caused them and told her not to touch him. She was so upset that she came over right away to tell me, even though she didn't want to drag me into it. You know how protective she's always been of his big fat ego."

"So? He was nervous and upset about all that's been going on in that godawful town for the past few years. If I lived there, I'd have a permanent case of hives. I used to get rashes all the time as a kid, remember?"

"I'm serious, Mickie. This is different. Let me tell you the rest. After the hives went away, he started rolling up the bedspread and putting it between them. Your mother didn't

91

know what was happening, and she was afraid to say anything. Every time she tried, he found fault with what she said, no matter what. She's been a nervous wreck for two months. What do you think of that?"

"What does Lola think of it?" Miguel looked blankly at his godmother. She faltered.

"Oh, you know. She never says anything." There was a long silence. Fine, spicy aromas were reaching them from the kitchen.

Miguel sensed that she knew what all of them had known for a long time and had come to protect her sister, to be on hand if something happened during the visit. His childhood adoration for her returned in a rush. Despite her stubborn nature, which was formidable and for which she had paid dearly, discretion and compassion were great forces in her soul. He felt anger toward Tony for having drowned himself.

"Nina," he decided to be direct. "It's very simple and you know it. Everybody knows it. Guilt has caught up with him, and he can't stand it any more."

She beamed. "You're a wise child," she said as she embraced him. "Let's eat. I'm starving." Leading him to the meal she had prepared, she added in a confiding tone, "After dinner I want to tell you about the spirits. You'll never believe what I've seen."

"Right," he said.

"Don't make fun, Mickie. You just won't allow yourself to see how psychic you are."

Now, faced with an uncontrollably weeping father, Miguel Chico didn't feel very psychic. He could only look on his father's pain in an abstract way, and he knew enough not to touch him. Years before, helping him pack in the middle of the night for his journey to Los Angeles to attend his brother Armando's funeral, Miguel Chico had attempted to comfort his father. It was the first time he had seen Miguel Grande cry and, still a child, he had reached out to him.

"Don't do that," his father had said, pushing him away. "Men don't do that with each other. Let me cry by myself. Go away."

The rebuff had hurt him and he had remembered the lesson. There was some vindictiveness in the impersonal tone he now used.

"What's the matter, Dad?"

"I'm in love with Lola, and I have to tell your mother about it."

"Don't you think she knows already?"

"Maybe, but not from me, and I have to tell her."

"Why? What will change if you do?"

"I don't know. I just can't stand the way things are now. It's getting to me pretty bad."

"Won't telling her make it worse? Unless you're going to tell her that you're leaving her to marry Lola. Is that what you want to do?"

"I don't know. I can't decide. I love them both so much. I want them to be one person."

"Well, they're not. And you've got to decide."

His father's tears continued in steady lines down his face, but the ugly, choking sounds had subsided. "I can't make up my mind. You are your mother's favorite. How do you feel about my leaving her and marrying Lola?"

"Make the decision first and then ask me."

Above them, in the living room, they could hear the sounds of the women. Miguel Chico was struck with a strong desire to know what they were talking about.

"Can they hear us?" his father asked, panic-stricken.

The look on Miguel Grande's face made his son hate

him more than ever. "Don't worry," he said angrily, "they can't hear anything."

Then Miguel Chico did not know what to say. He had always felt that his father disliked him for being too delicate, too effeminate. Miguel Grande had consistently refused to acknowledge that his son's feelings and needs might be different from his own, and he had thus failed to help the boy understand life. Because he had not looked at himself or others truly, the son could see no way of helping him now. Miguel Chico did not want the responsibility of his father's guilt; he had guilts enough of his own.

"What does Lola say about your leaving her best friend?" Miguel Chico began to feel the exhilaration of cruelty, of being able to injure as one has felt injured.

He carefully avoided saying "mother," knowing the very word would rekindle his father's jealousy over Juanita's deep and abiding love for her son. Years ago, upon learning of the Oedipus complex, Miguel Chico had savored the intuitive knowledge that his father was no rival for his mother's affections. It was clear to both mother and son that Miguel Grande at his most brutal could not break into their intricately woven web of feeling for each other.

His father's greatest strategic error in the losing battle to take precedence over his son in Juanita's esteem had occurred in the ninth year of their marriage. Many children were dying of polio, and he had refused to let Juanita take Miguel Chico, then eight, to the doctor.

"He's only being a brat," Miguel Grande said to her. "I overheard him on the phone saying he was pretending to be sick so that he wouldn't have to go to school."

"He loves school," Juanita replied. "I'm going to call the doctor for an appointment."

"I'm the head of this family, and you're not calling

anybody. I won't have you spoil him any more. You've already taken him away from me."

Juanita did not understand her husband, but she obeyed him. During the following weekend, Miguel Chico complained of backaches and a strange fatigue. Awakening from a nap, he experienced a moment of horror because it was growing darker rather than lighter outside. He wandered into the kitchen to ask about it. "It's five in the afternoon, not five in the morning, Mickie," his mother said. "How do you feel?" He did not answer but instead looked out at the darkness of the late September dusk, recognizing the same sense of doom and fear he had felt when Maria told him about the end of the world.

The following morning he got up and dressed for school, but he could not bend over to tie his shoes. Juanita tied them for him. He went to school but could not concentrate. At lunchtime his mother phoned from work and told him to take a bus downtown and meet her at the doctor's office as soon as school was out. A stranger carried him off the bus and to the doctor's office before Juanita arrived.

Until she was told that only his leg was affected and that he would have a slight limp for the rest of his life, Juanita thought her son was going to die. "It's all your fault," she said to her husband.

A few weeks later, after Miguel Chico was out of the hospital, Miguel Grande accused her of screaming the words at him in front of everyone at the doctor's office. "I didn't scream at all. You thought I was yelling because you knew I was right." Their son's illness caused a breach between them that no one, least of all Miguel Chico, knew how to mend.

If later he made excuses to himself and others for his behavior toward his oldest son, Miguel Grande never forgave himself. But neither could he bring himself to express his regret to Miguel Chico. It pained him to see his son walk, and eventually he invented ways to make a man of the adolescent boy. One device had been to ask Miguel Chico's school friends to engage him in fistfights so that he might learn to defend himself. Another was to enroll him in advanced swimming classes at the YMCA with private instructions to the teacher to be harder on him than on the other boys his age. All of his attempts failed because Juanita found out about them and protected her son even more vigilantly. Miguel Chico ignored his body and became a good student.

"You've ruined him," Miguel said to Juanita. She did not answer.

Now the ruined son faced his father. "What does Lola think about this?" Miguel Chico asked again.

"I haven't said anything to her yet."

"Shouldn't you? Won't she have something to say about it?"

"She'll do whatever I say. She's not like your mother." The strategy of suggesting that Juanita was to blame for being a disobedient female had puzzled Miguel Chico until he learned that his father had used it whenever he had something important to hide.

Traditionally the talk between him and his father had never gone beyond Miguel Grande's questioning and his replies. Their physical contact had been limited to a slap in the face or a bone-crushing hug that lacked affection and had been his father's way of showing that at middle-age he was still physically fit. Thus, Miguel Grande's desperation in coming to him was not lost on Miguel Chico.

"Are you sure of that? She doesn't look like a meek woman to me. She never has."

The tears began anew. Miguel Chico began to taste his father's blood.

"Women are shit, you know that? Why do you live alone?"

Miguel Chico remained silent. He felt his own manliness in choosing not to answer his father; it was his turn to question.

"She doesn't want you to leave Mother, does she?"

"She doesn't know what she wants. She wants me to tell her. She's forcing me to tell her."

"How?" The son used the knife as if it had been in his hands forever.

"I keep finding her with other men and it's tearing my guts out. I've even caught her with your godfather." The arid, strangling noises returned.

Miguel Chico had learned to believe only some of what his father said. Lola probably was sleeping with other men, but she was not calculating enough to try to force his father's hand, particularly when her friendship with Juanita was at stake. She did it for pure pleasure and because she loved giving herself to as many men as pleased her. He did not believe the part about his godfather Ernesto. It was another lie to make the people he loved seem as low as his father felt himself to be. Because of his father, Miguel Chico would never trust another man to tell him the truth about anything. His father's sins, visited upon him, helped and hurt him with the rest of the world. He would have preferred a life in which trust rather than suspicion guided his thoughts and actions.

His father looked at him stupidly. "You've got to make a decision, Dad. The one thing that's clear is that you're breaking down."

"Never happen," he said, wiping his face and blowing his nose.

There was no help for him. "Do you think you'll be all

right now? They'll wonder what's taking us so long."

Miguel Grande watched his son walk out of the room, then followed to join the women upstairs in the dining room. After dinner, they played cards in a joyless attempt to ignore the tension. Miguel Chico began to feel an aversion toward Lola and his parents that abated when his father announced that they were leaving the following day.

"But we just got here," Juanita said.

"We are leaving tomorrow," Miguel Grande said impatiently without looking at her. They returned to the desert.

As Juanita listened to her husband tell her in a voice strained with shame that he was in love with Lola, she looked at him in the same way she had looked at her father when he behaved badly toward her or Nina. She had long ago accepted Miguel's weakness for other women, and as she heard the sounds of his humiliation, she pitied him without anger. Fighting the impulse to hold him—she knew that to do so would hurt his pride—she sat staring at his pain, not yet aware of her own.

Her tears came from another source, deeper than the shame of the one man she had known intimately. She recalled being aware of her sexuality for the first time while bathing with Nina, who was too young to have hair on her body. Looking down at herself, Juanita had noticed a darkness there that shocked her. She had attempted to rub it out with the soap and washcloth, her back to her sister, ashamed to be seen touching herself. She knew with dreadful certainty that her father would punish her for that darkness, though how he would find out or how she would bring herself to tell him did not occur to her. She rubbed herself sore and wept secretly until she discovered from her aunt that such growth was natural. She wept because she could not understand the forces that drove men. They remained mysterious creatures to her, given either to tyrannizing others or to indulging themselves to distraction at the expense of others.

"Please don't cry," Miguel said to her.

"I can't help it. I'm crying because I miss Lola already." Saying her name, Juanita evoked her presence in the room where they had all sat together so many times. "And it makes me mad that I miss her. I know you have no shame, but she was my friend and I trusted her."

Miguel did not understand her. He felt only his pain in having to hurt her.

When Miguel first met Juanita, she was seeing someone else whom she was rumored to love. He courted her anyway because he responded to her innocence and to his own desire to teach her about the world. She was not easy prey, and she did not use the usual devices the other girls employed when they played at refusing his attention.

"Give me a little kiss," he said to her on their first date.

"No."

"Why? Didn't you like the show?" He had sat through it patiently knowing that she enjoyed musical extravaganzas. He liked them when the girls showed their legs.

"Yes, I did. Very much. Thanks."

"Then why don't you kiss me?"

"Because I don't want to."

Her manner, the complete lack of flirtation in her voice, her total indifference to the game of sex, surprised him and filled him with admiration. She was unreachable and incorruptible in the same ways as his mother, though he did not make the comparison then, or ever, but only presumed that she would be the mother of his children.

"What are you going to do now?" Juanita asked Miguel.

"I don't know."

"Why don't you go away for a few weeks and think about it?" She did not know where such words came from; she was saying whatever came into her head. Beneath the words, she felt panic beginning to undo her.

"Does that mean you don't want me to come back?"

"No. It means you have to decide what you're going to do." It did not seem to occur to him that he could not continue in the same way with both of them now.

"I don't know where to go."

"Oh, Miguel, how could you?" Anger was beginning to mix readily with her fear and pity.

"I don't know."

"I'm going to talk to Lola."

"No," he said quickly, "I don't want you to talk to her. Leave her alone, and tell all your friends who have been phoning her up and calling her names to leave her alone too." The lost child in him vanished in his defense of Lola, which gave Juanita the courage she needed.

"I'm not staying in this house tonight. I'm going over to Nina's. You do whatever you want."

She packed an overnight case, and before she walked out the front door she heard him turn on the television set in the den. She fought a desire to smash it to pieces. When she arrived at Nina's house, she lost control of herself.

When she was finally able to talk, Juanita said to her sister, "I hope you haven't been one of the people phoning her up."

"No, but now when I see her, I won't have to choke on my words. I can ignore her completely."

"Why didn't anyone tell me?"

"We tried, but you wouldn't listen."

"Poor Lola." She allowed herself to say her friend's name as a way of testing her feelings. Something important was being decided.

Nina became impatient. "What do you mean 'poor Lola'? That bitch has been taking advantage of you for a long time. And as for that husband of yours, it's about time you got rid of him. He's a liar and worse than a two-timer. I bet he's been giving her money and presents all this time. She's got a reputation for that, you know."

Juanita put her hand over her sister's mouth. "Nina, Nina, we have to understand each other about this," she said very carefully, as if the words were forming her future. "You are very stubborn and you bear grudges. Didn't losing Antony teach you anything at all? If you are going to be of any help to me in this, you have to promise that you will never again speak about Lola and Miguel like that. She is my friend and he is my husband and what has happened to the three of us is terrible and I am part of it. If you are going to make it worse, I won't talk to you about it. I need you, Nina. Help me with this, please."

Nina put her arms around her. After a while she said, "I'll do whatever you want."

Juanita went to bed in the room that would have been Tony's and that Nina insisted on furnishing with his things. In the middle of the night she awoke feeling like an orphan, dressed, left a note for Nina, and drove back to her own house. There was a light on in the kitchen and a note saying that Miguel was staying at the Y and would call her. She felt better at home and remained awake until dawn. Then she

101

read the morning paper, took her bath, and went to work as usual. No one asked about her eyes, and at noon Miguel phoned. His voice was weak and tired.

"I'm going to stay at the Y for a few days. I'll let you know where I'll be after that."

"Fine," she said. "Bring over your dirty clothes. I'll take care of them for you." The thought of his being alone was unbearable to her.

After Juanita had left for Nina's house, Miguel had driven to Lola's. When he told her what he had done, she reacted unexpectedly. "What's going to happen?" she asked, and she repeated the question often enough during the evening to annoy him. He tried spending the night with her, but his nervousness made her uncomfortable and irritable. He stayed at the Y a few days and then drove through the desert for a week. Lola had also suggested that he go away for a while, which made him suspect that the women were in league against him. He asked Lola if she had talked to Juanita.

"No, what do you take me for?" she replied angrily. His love for her returned. She was his woman.

"Let's go to Los Angeles," he said.

"No, you need to be by yourself." She had never before refused outright to do his bidding, and she quickly saw her error, adding, "I want to go, but I can't get out of work right now. You go, Miguel. You need the rest." She kissed his ear. "It will help you to be away from both of us."

But during the days of driving and smoking through endless miles of desert, he felt betrayed. She had not responded unequivocally. She had not appeared ready to abandon everything for him as he had expected and as he thought he was ready to do for her. He cried when he thought of Juanita. Her helplessness without him caused him to miss her more.

When Miguel returned to her Juanita welcomed him back with open arms. She promised herself to learn what pleased him in bed and to devote more of her free time to him instead of to friends and social activities. But she noticed that his face grew sad whenever certain songs played on the radio, and after a while she grew tired of sitting with him in front of the tv set, cigarette smoke wafting about her, trying to make conversation during the commercials. They did not mention Lola.

After a few months, he started going out on Friday nights without telling her where he was going or when he would return. Usually he came back before dawn, but sometimes he would not return until late Saturday afternoon, saying that he had stopped at the Y to play a few games of handball. She continued to see to it that he ate well, and washed and ironed his clothes as diligently as before.

She planned outings for herself on Friday nights but found that she preferred staying home. It saved her the trouble of explaining Miguel's whereabouts to his relatives or to her friends, who asked about him regularly. Alone, she watched television for an hour, then read, then walked around the house, then sang to herself, then cried, then went to bed and tried to read herself to sleep.

Their weekends together suffered from his Friday night excursions. She missed Lola most of all on Saturday nights and Sundays, and to make herself feel better she tried to bring back memories of weekends spent with El Compa and Sara. Sometimes she was able to persuade Miguel to play casino with her, but those games ended when he accused her of trying to make him feel guilty. Slowly, they slipped into a routine in which there always seemed to be a missing part. At the regular poker games, Miguel consistently annoyed everyone by playing "the widow" whenever it was his turn to deal. Nina bit her tongue and never mentioned Lola's name in their presence, and she listened quietly whenever Juanita talked about how much she missed her friend. She noticed, however, that her sister was beginning to behave like a martyr. She held her tongue.

On Friday nights, friends called to tell Juanita that Miguel's car was parked around the corner from Lola's house. She thanked them for their concern and felt a great weariness set in. One day Nina said to her, "You sure look tired all the time, *hermana*. Are you all right?"

"Yes, fine. Why?"

"Nothing. You just look tired all the time."

"All right, Nina. Say it."

"I don't want to say anything that will make you mad at me. I just don't like the way you've been acting lately. You're turning into one of those old ladies who do nothing but suffer, and usually because of some man. You haven't started complaining about your health or wearing black all the time, but I see it coming."

Juanita laughed. She was too tired to protest.

"I'm serious," Nina went on. "Is that what you want to be? Why don't you talk to her? You and the whole town know that he goes over there every Friday night. Why don't you go over with him and have a good long talk with both of them. Get it over with, one way or another."

"I can't do that." The thought of such a confrontation filled her with dread. "He wouldn't allow it. And I haven't spoken to her since he told me about it. What would I say?"

"You'll think of something."

As she approached the door of Lola's house the following Friday, shortly after a friend had called to say that Miguel had arrived, Juanita prayed for the courage not to cry in front of them. Miguel came to the door and let her in without a word. He barely seemed surprised. Lola was sitting on the sofa with a drink in her hand. She looked thinner, but her skin was lovelier than ever and her eyes greeted Juanita with a warmth that showed through her guilt and fear.

"Juanita, how are you?"

"Fine, Lola. Long time no see."

"Yes, it has been a long time."

"May I sit down?"

"Of course."

"The three of us need to talk."

Miguel remained silent as the women discussed their situation.

"If you want him, Lola, you can have him," Juanita began. He was stunned. In the end the women agreed that he was a liar, that he must choose between them, and that they were sorry for the hurt they had caused each other. Lola kept having to excuse herself with apologies for the weakness of her stomach, but she saw it through to the end. In her absence, Juanita ignored Miguel altogether. She did not cry.

After Juanita left, Lola told Miguel that since her son had just bought a house large enough to accommodate her and his family, she thought she might move to Los Angeles. She needed time by herself, she said, and asked Miguel not to spend the night. He went to the Y.

He stayed there for a week, astonished by the women's behavior. Lola had not remained loyal to him in the crisis, but he did not believe she would leave town and begin a new life without him. And Juanita had not seemed at all helpless. Her disregard for him reminded him of his mother.

He returned to Juanita, and Lola made plans to move. Out of pride and because of the way she had behaved in front of Juanita, he refused to see her. Three months later, on the day before she left, she phoned Juanita.

"May I come over and say goodbye to you, Lola?"

"Oh, Juanita, what for?"

"I'll tell you when I see you. I'll be there in half an hour."

When she returned, Miguel was waiting for her. He was still scoffing at Lola's plans and firmly believed that she would be back. Her departure, he reasoned, would give her an excuse to sell at a profit the house she and El Compa had lived in together. Then when she returned, she would be able to set herself up in a nice apartment and make everything easier for him.

"Where have you been?" he asked his wife casually.

"Lola's. I went to tell her goodbye. I won't be seeing her for a long time."

"She'll be back."

"I don't think so, Miguel."

After a few moments, he said, "You were there a long time."

"We had a lot to say to each other."

"Oh? What?"

"I'm not going to tell you." She never told anyone, not even Nina.

When he realized almost a year later that Lola was not coming back, Miguel went to Los Angeles twice to see her. The first time he told himself that he was leaving Juanita for good, that nothing had changed, that she was still more devoted to others than to him. True, their sex life had improved and she no longer made him feel that he was hurting her all the time, but no experience could be like sleeping with Lola.

Without letting him know, Juanita understood and accepted Miguel's constant desire for Lola. In her brooding, she decided that even if the experience of a great sexual passion had been denied her, a lasting relationship based on such intense feelings survived only in the movies and bestsellers that she loved. It could not survive daily life. She felt less awed by Lola's physical power and began, instead, to pity her. She thought Lola was brave to have moved away, yet it pained her that they would never be together again as in the old days.

Miguel's first trip to Los Angeles, however, shocked her. They had been to a dance sponsored by her club of Mexican women. Miguel referred to them as "the hippos" because they all weighed more than one hundred and sixty-five pounds, but he enjoyed teasing them and trading obscene stories. At the dance he behaved in an unusually courteous manner and even conversed politely with friends and relatives she knew he disliked. They danced every dance together, and she felt pride in demonstrating to them all that she had been able to hold onto her man.

When they got home, they made love. But his silence unnerved her, and while washing herself she listened for signs of discontent. The silence from the bedroom alerted her.

"Anything wrong?" she asked as naturally as she could. He was smoking.

"I'm going to L.A. tomorrow. I have to see her. I'm already packed and I want to get away before six." "

It took her a few minutes to rally.

"But why? Why do you want to bother her now? Leave her alone, Miguel. I thought you were happy again."

"I have to see her," he said.

She did not reply. In the morning she prepared breakfast for him, ironed two of his better dress shirts, and, repacking his valise, folded them neatly so that they would not be too wrinkled when he needed them. "It's almost the holidays," she said. "Do you have to go now?"

"Yes," he said.

They were both defeated. After he left, she returned to bed and fought against her bitterness. She, too, had missed Lola terribly and wanted to see her.

Miguel was gone a month, and because of the Christmas festivities and family gatherings it was an especially difficult time for Juanita. She did not know if Miguel would return in time. When she telephoned Miguel Chico to tell him, he said he would not be able to visit after all but encouraged her to spend the holidays in San Francisco. She refused. She lost courage and indulged in fits of weeping and despair.

"I told you," Nina said two days before Christmas, "your husband is no good."

"Shut up," Juanita said sharply. But she was beginning to believe it. She wrote Miguel a letter in care of Lola's son telling him how disappointed she was in him and that when he returned, as she knew he would, he had better make plans to live elsewhere, because she did not want him in her house. She ended by saying that they ought to think seriously about separating. It was an angry letter and she did not let herself reread it for fear she might repent and not send it.

The day after mailing it, she received a bouquet of flowers from him with a long note saying he now realized that he loved her more than anyone else. Their letters had crossed, and when he returned after the holidays she let him in.

The following autumn, he told her that he was driving to California for the World Series.

"That's good," she said, "when are you leaving?"

"Day after tomorrow."

"I'll get your things ready."

Her tone surprised him. No questions, no tears,

complete obedience. She knew he would see Lola, but it did not seem to matter to her. She did not even ask when he would be back. He returned five days later, and when he walked into the bedroom she looked up from her book and asked if he had enjoyed himself.

"Sort of."

"How is she?"

"Okay. She told me to give you her love."

"That's nice," Juanita answered without sarcasm or irony.

He could not bring himself to tell her the truth. Lola had been angry with him for arriving unannounced. They had spent only one evening together, had gone through the motions of lovemaking, and as he left, she had said, "Miguel, call before you come the next time, will you? And give my love to Juanita. Tell her I miss her very much."

That Christmas, Juanita received a card from Lola.

Dear Juanita!

Thank you for your beautiful card. It touched me deeply, and all I can say is that you are absolutely incredible. I do believe you. I feel the same way about you, and it isn't because it's that time of year. I've always felt that way. At one time I was very bitter because my name was being smeared all over, but that's over. Whatever happened, I had coming. Someday, I hope I can get everything off my chest. I know it's going to hurt, but we've all been hurt so much before, maybe it won't be that bad. I know it's a hell of a time to tell you this, but I'm feeling brave, so please forgive me. I love you and Miguel very much.

Lola

Juanita showed the card to Miguel Chico, home for the holiday. "What did you say in your note to her?" he asked.

"Oh, I don't remember. You know, the usual."

He liked it when she dissembled. It was very uncharacteristic of her and he especially liked that she enjoyed feigning indifference to Lola.

"Mickie," she said, "please try not to fight with your father this time."

"You're starting again, Mother."

"What?"

"To be a mother. Stop it, I'm too old. I don't like him and he doesn't like me."

"He loves you. He just doesn't know how to show it very well. But you know he'd do anything for you."

"Right."

"He's been very good to me in these last months."

"That's wonderful, Mother. It's good to know you're happier now. Remember last Christmas?"

"Don't remind me. That's all over and I'm happy now." She stopped setting the table. "Except."

"Except what?"

"I wish El Compa were alive and that he and Lola were here with us. Remember those times?"

"Oh, Mother, you are impossible. Didn't you ever feel like telling her to go to hell?"

"No."

"You're too good to be true."

Juanita laughed. "Tell that to your father."

RAIN DANCER

F elix Angel, Mama Chona's oldest son, was murdered by an eighteen-year-old soldier from the South on a
cold, dry day in February. They were in Felix's car in a desert canyon on the eastern side of the mountain, and they
talked only briefly before the boy kicked him to death. Because of the mountain and the shadows it casts, it was already twilight in the canyon, but on the western side where
Felix lived the sun was still setting in those bleak, final moments when he thought of his family and, in particular, of
his youngest and favorite son, JoEl.

The border town where Felix spent most of his life is
in a valley between two mountain ranges in the middle of the
southwestern wastes. A wide river, mostly dry except when
thunderstorms create flashfloods, separates it from Mexico.
Heavy traffic flows from one side of the river to the other,
and from the air, national boundaries and differences are
indistinguishable.

Imagining his uncle's last moments while sitting in his study gazing out at the California dusk settling on the leaves of the birch tree and turning them blue, Miguel Chico felt the sadness of that time of day. There are no sounds in the desert twilight. On very cold or very hot days, the land and its creatures breathe in that dry acid air of the space between day and night and, as the first stars appear, resume their activities in one long exhalation. Felix loved those quiet moments at dusk as much as the smell of the desert just before and after a thunderstorm when the sky, charged with lightning, became fresh with the fragrance of the mesquite, greasewood, and vitex trees. He had never been able to describe the smell until one day JoEl, not yet five years old, had said, "They're coming. I smell them."

"Who? What are you talking about?"

"The angels."

"You mean the family?" Felix asked.

"No. The ones in the sky."

From then on, JoEl could tell them when it was going to rain.

When Felix was a child he would run outside and dance when the storm clouds passed over, while his brothers and sisters hid under the bed. Neither Mama Chona, nor later his own family, could stop him.

"You'll be struck by lightning," they said.

"Good. I'll die dancing."

Felix and the young soldier had met in a bar around the corner from the courthouse. The bar serves minors and caters to servicemen and has enough of an ambiguous reputation to be considered an interesting or suspicious place by the townspeople on the "American" side of the river. Usually, afraid to be seen in such places, the citizens north of the river went to the dives and nightclubs across the border in search of release or fantasy and returned to their homes refreshed, respectability intact, like small-town tourists a little hung over after a week in New York or San Francisco.

But Mama Chona's son Felix was not a respectable man. Constantly on the lookout for the shy and fair god who would land safely on the shore at last, Felix searched for his youth in obscure places on both sides of the river. He went to the servicemen's bar regularly after work at the factory. On payday he treated everyone to a round of drinks, talked and laughed in jolly ways, and offered young soldiers a ride to the base across town, especially when he paid visits to his mother's sister, Tia Cuca, out in the desert.

Felix had been irritable that day because of his argument with JoEl at the breakfast table. Ordinarily he approached his work and even the difficult disputes between laborers and bosses with a casual good humor his comrades at the plant appreciated. He had been a graveyard shift laborer when his daughters, Yerma and Magdalena, were very young, but after Roberto and JoEl were born he was promoted to regular shift foreman. In the last five years he had been put in charge of hiring cheap Mexican workers. He had accepted the promotion on the condition that these men immediately be considered candidates for American citizenship and had been surprised when the bosses agreed. After thirty-five years, he was content with his work at the factory.

The Mexicans he hired reminded Felix of himself at that age, men willing to work for any wage as long as it fed their families while strange officials supervised the preparation of their papers. As middleman between them and the promises of North America, he knew he was in the loathsome position of being what the Mexicans called a *coyote*; for that reason he worked hard to gain their affection.

A person of simple and generous attachments, Felix

loved these men, especially when they were physically strong and naive. Even after losing most of his own hair and the muscles he had developed during his early years on the job, he had not lost his admiration for masculine beauty. As he grew older that admiration, instead of diminishing as he had expected, had become an obsession for which he sought remedy in simple and careless ways.

Before they were permitted to become full-time employees, the men were required to have physical examinations. These examinations, Felix told them, were absolutely necessary and, if done by him, were free of charge. He scheduled appointments for them at his sister Mema's place across the river. The physical consisted of tests for hernias and prostate trouble and did not go beyond that unless the young worker, awareness glinting at him with his trousers down, expressed an interest in more. The opportunists figured that additional examinations might be to their advantage, though Felix did not take such allowances into account later. In those brief morning and afternoon encounters, gazing upon such beauty with the wonder and terror of a bride, his only desire was to touch it and hold it in his hands tenderly. The offended, who left hurriedly, were careful to disguise their disgust and anger for fear of losing their jobs. He could not find words to assure them. In most cases, however, the men submitted to Felix's expert and surprisingly gentle touch, thanked him, and left without seeing the awe and tension in his face. It did not occur to them that another man might take pleasure in touching them so intimately.

Later, after the men were secure in their work, the more aware among them joked about the *examinaciones* and winked at each other when Felix passed by on his way in and out of the office. None but the most insecure harbored ill will toward him, because his kindness, of which they took advantage on days when they were inexcusably late or absent, was known to all. A few, feigning abdominal pains, returned for more medical care and found themselves turned away. Most forgot the experience, occasionally referred to him behind his back but affectionately as *Jefe Joto*, and were grateful for the extra money he gave them for the sick child at home.

On the day of his morning argument with JoEl, Felix had not responded to any of his men in the usual friendly manner. In an attempt to tease him out of his mood, one of them talked loudly about the phases of the moon. Felix stared at the man.

"Hey, *Jefe*, it was only a joke." The young Mexican pronounced the English "j" like a "y" and Felix said to him angrily, "Hey, *pendejo*, why don't you stop being a stupid wetback and learn English?" Then, murmuring an apology, he walked toward the man as if to embrace him, gave him a strange look, and walked away.

Any disagreement with JoEl caused Felix to be irritated with everyone, even his wife Angie toward whom he felt the kind of tenderness one has for a creature one loves and injures accidentally. He was unbearably ashamed of his remarks to the young laborer. Alone in his office at the noon hour, eating the burritos Angie had prepared for him, he choked on his shame.

The beer at the bar was good enough to restore his spirits and it began to give him the calm he needed to mull over his quarrel with JoEl. Felix loved young people and did not understand why his son did not see that. Now that JoEl was fourteen and more rebellious than ever, their arguments became nightmares during which Felix said words he did not mean. JoEl replied in curt, distant phrases that cut him off and caused anger to rise from his belly into his throat with a vehemence that caught him off guard. Their arguments never directly confronted the deeper antagonism that had begun to grow between them. Sometimes, even without speaking to each other, the tension was so palpable that one of them was forced to leave the room.

"But I want to go on that trip," JoEl had said harshly.

"I don't have the money to give you for it," Felix answered in the same tone.

"You have the money for beer and for Lena whenever she wants it."

"Your sister is older than you and needs it for important things, not for football trips with gringos." Felix liked gringos and football. Why had he said that?

"Oh, yeah," JoEl replied, "important things, huh? Like a phony pearl necklace for her date with that *pachuco* she's been seeing."

"He's not a *pachuco*. He plays in the band she sings with, and it's important for her to look nice. She's got talent."

"She's got talent, all right." JoEl's face had been ugly when he repeated the word.

—My beautiful son, don't look like that. It will wrinkle your face like a prune and your eyes will harden and break my heart.

Felix saw JoEl's eyes floating in the warm darkness of the bar. He would borrow money from his younger brother Miguel Grande, who would lend it without any questions or conditions. Felix felt the cold air of the desert winter as someone came into the bar, but the glare from the light outside blinded him so that he saw only the silhouette of a young man in uniform cross the threshold. JoEl's eyes disappeared into the far corner of the room.

Felix and his first son Roberto did not quarrel. Berto, who was Angie's favorite, was happy and easygoing—not a thinker like JoEl—and they all enjoyed his company. He helped his father fix the car whenever anything went wrong with it and would talk to him quietly about his problems with girls. He was dark-skinned like his mother, very "Indian," polite and shy. Felix returned his love in a steady, uncomplicated way. Only JoEl, antagonism causing his cinnamon eyes to seem darker, persistently disagreed with Felix about almost everything.

"You are just like your father," Angie told him. "Stubborn and too proud for your own good." She spoke English with a heavy Mexican accent and used it only when she wanted to make "important" statements, not realizing that her accent created the opposite effect. After his first year in school JoEl learned to be ashamed of the way his mother abused the language. The others, including Felix, loved to tease and imitate her. Their English was perfect and Spanish surfaced only when they addressed their older relatives or when they were with their Mexican school friends at social events.

"Come on, Mother, say it again," Magdalena pleaded.

"*No seas malcriada,*" Angie said and waved her hand close to Lena's cheek.

"No, Ma, not in Spanish. Say it in English." Lena and her summer boyfriend were on the front porch, seated side by side hardly touching, swinging slowly back and forth. Every night at exactly nine-thirty, Angie went to the screen door behind them and said, "Magdah-leen, kahm een." Lena shrieked with delight; the sad boyfriend smiled apprehensively.

"Oh, Mamá, just a few more minutes." She said "mamá" in the Spanish way.

"No, *señorita*. Joo mas kahm een rye now." More howls, as the boy said an embarrassed good night and slipped from the swing and the porch into the dark. Lena barely noticed. She was too taken up by her mother, whom she adored.

Of his two girls, Lena was more like his wife, small and dark, with eyes like JoEl's. From his room in the back on those hot desert nights, Felix loved hearing the women talk and laugh after the boyfriends left, and he followed them in his reveries before sleep as they walked arm in arm from the living room to the kitchen spraying mosquitoes and turning off lights.

Angie had painted the rooms brilliant colors to annoy Felix's sisters, knowing that Jesus Maria and Eduviges disapproved of her and thought her a "lower class Mexican." She had also chosen the colors for their names: *Perico Tropical* and *Sangrita del Rey*. Felix agreed to buy the paint because he could refuse her nothing and because he knew that she would keep her word and paint the rooms without anyone's help. Her daughters had long since despaired of teaching Angie the good taste they learned in their home economics classes at school.

"But Mother, the colors are too bright." Yerma, her older and more prudish daughter, was shocked as she walked in the door after school.

"I dun't care," Angie said in her best English. "I dun't like white rooms. They give me the suzie creeps."

"The what?"

"Joo know, the suzie creeps." When Yerma figured out that her mother had combined current slang with a French dessert, she was too amused to insist on a subdued version of the colors already drying on the walls. From then on, anything white they disliked gave them all the "suzie creeps." And Yerma, who secretly loved white, painted her own room a lighter version of the tropical parrot in the living room.

Angie and Lena walked through that room, then the purple dining room, and into the bright yellow kitchen to set the table for the next morning. Felix heard them getting ready for bed and fell asleep. Lena and Angie now slept in the same room, he and JoEl in the back porch they had walled in with cinder blocks, and Yerma in the front bedroom on the double bed where all but she had been conceived. Berto slept on the living room sofa. When JoEl was ten Felix bought him a bed of his own, but until then they had slept together.

From the time he was very young, JoEl had dreamed vividly. He had often come to his parents' bed and stayed there until at dawn he fell asleep out of fatigue, his terror diminished by the light and the warmth of his mother and father on either side of him. When his son's dreams were very bad, Felix learned not to ask him about them. Instead, he allowed JoEl to weep away his terror while he and Angie took turns rocking him. At first they had attempted to exorcise JoEl's demons by asking him to describe them, but they saw that this made him even more frightened and inconsolable. Gradually they arrived at the better solution, but it was difficult because his fear was monstrous in relation to his size and frightened them. The first time he awakened the household with his screams, Angie wept out of frustration because he could not tell her what he saw.

"JoEl, what's the matter? What is it? Tell me." It was clear that JoEl, eyes open, did not see her, and the more she begged him to name his monsters the louder he screamed.

He did name them once when he was just learning to speak. The week before, Yerma and Lena had been teaching him the words for bugs in Spanish and English. JoEl was fascinated by the sugar ants that created roadways in the kitchen every summer, and which Angie could never bring herself to poison. They had begun crawling over his legs as he sat on the floor observing them, and only Yerma saw that he was hypnotized by fear and not curiosity. She could tell by the color of his face, pale yellow with a blue cast under the eyes, which was also its color during his nightmares. She brushed the ants from his legs, saying their diminutive Spanish name, "*Hormiguitas, hormiguitas,* JoEl," and tickling him at the base of his spine in an attempt to make him laugh. He neither laughed nor cried, but the natural color returned to his face.

"*Moleecas,*" he had said, "*moleecas.*"

Yerma smiled. "Not *moleecas. Hor-mi-gui-tas.*" She kissed him.

"*Moleecas,*" he had repeated seriously.

Sitting up in bed in the desert night, frantically brushing over his legs and arms in rigid, measured gestures that awed the family as they stood around him, JoEl screamed, "*Moleecas.*"

Watching him, Felix's heart broke with the knowledge that his son was a poet. He motioned Angie not to touch him until the gestures stopped and the eyes lost their unearthly sheen. He then lifted JoEl from the cot with great tenderness and took him to their bed.

As the three of them slept more frequently together, Felix lost his passion for Angie, and he would wake during the night cradling JoEl on his side of the bed. His protective feelings for the child perplexed and disoriented him because they seemed stronger than his desire for his wife. In the beginning, Angie paid no attention and was touched deeply by Felix's love for their son. Slowly, without intending it, she stifled her own desires and lay awake watching her husband and son in their timeless embrace. In the summer the crickets kept her company and in the winter she listened to the wind.

Finally, she set up the cot for herself in Lena's room, helped Yerma move their double bed into the front room when she started high school, and never disturbed Felix again. "He's a good man," she confessed to her priest in Spanish. "I have my children, my house, enough to eat. What more do I need?" The priest said nothing.

She remained thin and small with the beautiful arms of a medieval madonna, but she forgot to dye her hair at times and laughed with the irony of the sexually deprived. Her own desire for Felix cooled and, loving both her husband and son, she knew her son's strength and sided with her husband whenever they quarreled.

Felix ordered another beer as a North American ballad the children liked to sing began playing on the jukebox. Yerma, Lena, and JoEl had good voices and serenaded him and Angie often, though lately JoEl had stopped joining in.

He and his son began to quarrel after JoEl had been in school for two years. "Leave me alone," JoEl had said to him one evening when Felix tried to see what he was reading. "Can't I have any privacy in this house?" The whole idea was preposterous to Felix, as he was not prepared to believe that his youngest child could understand the full meaning of those words in English or Spanish. The more Felix hounded him, the more JoEl retreated into his private world of books. Felix knew he was wrong to be envious of that world, but he could not help himself.

"JoEl, you read too much. You're going to ruin your eyes. Let's go for a ride." He had just bought a new Chevrolet. JoEl did not look up from his book.

Their fights wounded Angie most of all, and Felix saw how careful she was not to intrude. She watched them, however, ready to spring between him and JoEl when Felix's frustration led him to begin undoing his belt. After those occasions, when he and Angie sat alone in the kitchen, she attempted to soothe him by talking to him quietly. She told him that she hid from JoEl's laughter when the belt buckle struck him. Only later, when she heard the boy crying to himself, was she reassured that they had not lost him. She understood that a father's pride did not allow him to apologize to his son, but couldn't he allow JoEl some freedom to do what he wanted?

"What freedom?" Felix asked her in Spanish. "Freedom to turn into a delinquent or to become a selfish little brat? He belongs to a family and he must learn to share. I know what they're teaching kids in those schools. How to disobey parents and how to act like grownups when they're only children. And they also teach them to be ashamed of where they come from."

Angie defended JoEl by reminding Felix that he was only eleven years old, very intelligent, and most of the time a good son. But even while defending him, Angie agreed with Felix about the schools. Unlike Berto and the girls, JoEl did not come to her for comfort. He disdained it from all of them, and she attributed his distance to the ideas he was learning from the younger Anglo teachers. When JoEl taunted her sarcastically for putting up with Felix's injustices, she did not understand what he was doing. They did not seem injustices to her but simply the rights of a husband and father. Her duty was to suffer from his arbitrary nature so that she might enjoy greater glory in heaven. JoEl scorned her for doing her duty. Felix noticed how icily JoEl looked at Angie after he had berated her for spending her household money in foolish ways.

"Don't look at your mother like that."

"I can look at her any way I want."

"Don't talk back to me."

"Why?"

JoEl's most effective tactic was silence. Wordlessly, he let Angie know that she deserved the pain she endured and that she was no better than a worm for letting Felix take advantage of her goodness.

"You have no respect for us," she said to him in self-defense. "*Malcriado, muchacho malcriado.*"

"Well, you brought me up," JoEl answered.

At this point if he was present, Felix undid his belt. "Don't talk to your mother like that."

But when the family was happy, the house sang and the sofa played music. Lena, who had perfect pitch, discovered that if you sat on it in a certain way, it played two notes. These they incorporated into the background music for their songs. Felix and JoEl laughed together in the old ways and the others became infected with their joy. After the evening meal, they sang for their parents the songs they learned in school. Angie understood that they were patriotic North American songs and praised and kissed her children even if she did not like the music.

Berto was a perfect audience because he liked everything they did. JoEl told them stories and riddles he had read or made up, or sometimes he recited poems which they pretended to understand. He made them feel sad and Angie would look at him and wonder what was to become of her youngest child. As he grew older and turned more to himself, her fears grew with him. Sadness stuck to JoEl like the smell of garlic, she said to Felix. There was no remedy. Neither lemon nor baking soda could reach his pain and she contemplated it while preparing the evening meal. This time of day—twilight—was the most melancholy time of the day to her. The aroma of the rice made her think of JoEl's poems. Felix watched her stir it as he hugged her from behind.

An old romantic Mexican ballad was playing on the jukebox now and reminded Felix of the days when he was courting Angie. As usual, the singer was suffering from love and Felix smiled at the sentimentality of the lyrics. "Ay, Papa, how can you listen to such corny music?" the children asked him at home. He was not ashamed to admit that he loved all music. He and Angie had danced to this song shortly before and after they were married. After three beers, he sang along.

"Hey, Felix," asked the bartender, "what does it mean?"

"You wouldn't understand, you stupid gringo," he said. To himself he thought how only a Mexican song could mix sadness and laughter like that so that one could cry and sing at the same time. Another beer came sliding down the counter toward him.

Felix and Angie had met at school. They were among the first large group of Mexicans (or, as their teachers referred to them, "first generation Americans") to graduate from the town's high school. He was an average student with an undisciplined talent for music and literature that was discovered too late by a teacher who liked his sense of humor. She recommended that he be allowed to take college preparation courses but was told by the head counselor that it was too late for him to enroll. She knew that it was not but did not argue, seeing that Felix's family circumstances would keep him from continuing his education. His family, though proud of him, expected him to find a job right away. His sisters were anxious to see him begin fulfilling his duty as family breadwinner, for their father had died when they first crossed the border and Mama Chona had suffered much to keep them all together. Jesus Maria and Eduviges were tired of the menial work they took on which interfered with their studies.

The week after he received his diploma, he announced to the family his intention to marry Angie. Only his youngest sister Mema shared his happiness and embraced him. His brothers were still too young to care very much one way or another. They had no desire to attend schools of any kind after their grammar school experiences and were looking forward to the day they could find jobs that would allow them to earn the money to buy a car.

Before she left the kitchen where they were all seated for lunch, Jesus Maria said to him, "How could you do this to us? After all the sacrifices we've made for you? Now you're going to marry that *India* and leave the burden of this household to us." Jesus Maria had light skin and anyone darker she considered an "Indian." She said she did not understand how Angie had even gotten through school. Obviously she belonged to that loathsome group of Indians who were herded through the system, taught to add at least since they refused to learn any language properly, and then let loose among decent people who must put up with their ignorance. Jesus Maria knew that her family was better than such illiterates and she would prove it by going on to college.

"Don't worry, Jessie, I'll still help. You'll see, we'll work things out." He tried to put his arms around her, but she pushed him away and left the room. Felix faced his mother now. Mama Chona had remained silent throughout her children's quarrel.

"Come here, son," she said to him in her refined Spanish. "Let me kiss you." He had not expected her to assent so readily. She stood up and continued to tell him that she wished his father were alive so that he could give Felix the family blessing. She, God forgive her, could not.

Felix watched his mother walk away from him, a small despair beginning to impinge on his love for Angie. "I don't need your blessing, Mamá," he said in English, knowing she understood. "With or without it, I'm going to marry her."

And he did, five years later, after he had gotten the job at the factory and all but Mema and Miguel Grande were graduated from high school. Yerma and Lena were born in the first two years of their marriage, Berto a year later and JoEl two years after him.

Mama Chona forgave Felix for marrying beneath him when she saw her granddaughter, for whom she would have felt unrestrained affection had Yerma's skin been lighter. Angie learned quickly not to be hurt by her mother-in-law's snobbery, but she did not like it when Mama Chona held Yerma in her arms and called her a little Indian. "Don't worry about it," Felix said to her. "It's just the pot calling the kettle black."

When Yerma was eight years old she began taking piano lessons from Mrs. Ramos, the wife of a wealthy boot manufacturer. She was a good pupil and her talent was recognized by all who heard her play on the old piano Tia Cuca had given them when she moved out to the desert on the other side of the mountain. When Mrs. Ramos raised her fee from fifty cents to two dollars an hour, Angie, who saved money for the lessons out of the household budget, was unable to afford the increase. She did not want to ask Felix for it because she knew he did not have it, so Yerma no longer made the weekly climb up the hill to the rich peoples' part of town. She began practicing on her own with a devotion that ignored how badly out of tune their piano was, and she relied on Lena's ear to tell her how it should sound. They commented on its steady decline. "Pretty soon, Yerma, we can transpose everything down a whole tone. I can't wait, my ears are killing me."

One afternoon, Angie took Yerma up to the Ramos mansion. They were met at the back door by one of the kitchen servants who led them to the music room on the ground floor. Angie, who had never been to the house because she was too ashamed of her clothes to attend the biannual recitals in the living room upstairs, almost lost her nerve in the face of so many beautiful things. She had not dreamed of such furniture, and she calculated that her entire house could fit easily into this lower level. "What beauty," she said out loud to Yerma.

They waited outside the music room in an alcove with windows looking out onto a garden filled with flowers. Angie could not believe they were real. "Imagine," she said, "in this desert." Yerma was afraid her mother would ask permission to touch them and was about to insist that they go home and not bother Mrs. Ramos, when her mother's attention focused upon the sofa. It was the most comfortable Angie had ever known, of a pale orchid color, and she dared not lean back for fear of sinking too far and disappearing altogether. Later, she said to Felix that in the Ramos mansion, everyone sat on clouds. Yerma was embarrassed by her mother's reactions and remained silent. She did not want Angie to plead with Mrs. Ramos for anything because she was afraid her teacher would then dislike her. At the same time, she did not want to hurt her mother's feelings by denying her the chance to bargain for the lessons. But she wished that her mother would behave differently, as one did in church, with respect and a certain lack of enthusiasm.

After all the students finished their lessons, Yerma and Angie were admitted to the music room. There were three pianos in it, two uprights and a baby grand. The students were allowed to play the magnificent full grand piano upstairs during dress rehearsals and recitals, and so four times a year Yerma lovingly touched the most beautiful object she had ever seen.

"Señora Ramos, I am Yerma's mother," Angie began confidently in Spanish. She counted on the inspiration she had prayed for to give her the necessary words, but instead there followed a long silence that made Yerma want to cry.

Mrs. Ramos responded kindly, "How happy I am to meet you, Señora Angel." To Yerma she expressed her happiness at seeing her again. "I've missed you," she said warmly.

Angie, encouraged, continued in Spanish. "Señora, my daughter has practiced every day and plays well. Please listen to her."

"Of course."

Yerma sat down quickly and played a simplified version of Chopin's "Minute Waltz" which she had mastered on her own. When she finished, Angie asked Mrs. Ramos what she thought.

"Thank you very much, Yerma, you played that very well. I'm glad you have been practicing. Please wait outside for a few minutes, I want to talk to your mother." Mrs. Ramos spoke in Spanish out of courtesy to Angie.

Afterward, Yerma told Felix that these were the most difficult moments for her. She felt ashamed yet happy that Mrs. Ramos had praised her technique, since she knew her to be a good teacher who meant what she said. A few minutes later Angie emerged from the music room, took her arm, and led her out of the house. As they walked down the hill her mother told her that she would begin her lessons again the following week, and they hurried home to give the good news to the rest of the family.

Now, after every visit to the mansion, Yerma came home to find JoEl sitting on the piano bench, waiting impatiently to learn what his sister had been taught by the mysterious lady who lived on the hill.

In the bar, Felix saw them sitting together on the bench, his oldest and youngest children, arguing and disagreeing about a phrase, humming the melodies out loud in key, and then playing them to each other on that sad old piano. He would borrow the money somehow to get it tuned for them. Food was not enough for his children. They needed music.

The beer, the ballads, and JoEl's eyes floating through the air began to act as a balm for the irritations of the day. He wished JoEl were outside waiting for him so that they might drive out to Tia Cuca's together. Felix could not believe that JoEl was irrevocably lost to him. Yet he knew it was so by the way Angie had looked at him several weeks before and said, "That's enough. Let him go." How could he? To what? Who would protect him from his nightmares and his melancholy? Felix peered into the darkness of the bar for the first time in an effort to locate the young man who had entered earlier. He saw only a string of small Christmas lights, sad remnants which acted as permanent illumination for the far side of the room. He returned to his beer.

The lights on the tree, which was scraggly and already dried out after only three days, pleased JoEl. Yerma and Lena had stopped bickering long enough to complete the decorating with angel's hair. It gave the lights a strange brightness that made JoEl think of heaven. He knew little about religion yet, but they had told him of heaven where he would go if he were good, and of a devil who would throw him in the fire if he were bad. He sat on the sofa in a trance while the girls finished their fussing over the tree and stood back to admire their work. Too big for them to pick up and hug and too small to help, he was content to sit and enjoy the colored lights made fuzzy by the synthetic cobwebs.

From the kitchen, the aroma of their mother's cooking reached them. She had worked a long time on the batter for the tamales, whipping it smooth and creamy so that its redolent corn smell made them want to eat it before it was cooked. "You're going to get sick," Angie always warned them, but sneaking tastes from the batter was worth the stomachache, even if it would cause your *ombligo* to burst. Your *ombligo* was where you were born, and to JoEl it was the most sacred part of the body. Often, when he was frightened or very happy, he would twist his finger in its hollow until he made small suction noises. He loved his *ombligo*.

They ate the tamales before midnight mass, which he was not yet allowed to attend. Yerma opened his and cut it for him so that he tasted the meat and red chile inside even before he put them in his mouth. He was the official family taster.

"Is it good, JoEl?" Angie stood over him and watched as he ate the first bites. His silence and the look on his face reassured her of her accomplishment. Everyone else commented on the lightness of the dough and the especially good flavor of the chile that year, or the tenderness of the meat Angie had saved every cent to purchase from the best butcher in town. Felix put his arms around her waist as she stood by him with more tamales and told her what a splendid cook she was. The children loved it when their parents touched each other in front of them. Angie, of course, was able to find fault with her cooking. "Next year, they'll be better. You'll see," she said, trusting that the yellow-white corn husks which were more and more difficult to find would be available the following year. She could not imagine tamales without them.

In the morning, after the gifts were opened, Felix prepared *capirotada*. It was his annual rite in the kitchen where for the rest of the year Angie reigned. JoEl was the only member of the family permitted to watch his father prepare the rich bread pudding, and sensing the privilege from the beginning, he kept still as Felix chose the best slices of dried bread and cut them into perfect cubes.

They closely monitored the milk scalding on the stove, for if it overheated it would have to be thrown out and fresh milk brought in from the market. The brown sugar, the freshly grated nutmeg, the cinnamon lay waiting in small, carefully measured piles. They and the sherry beside them sent out fragrances that made JoEl drunk with pleasure. Sometimes their strength, particularly that of the nutmeg, made his head ache, a fact he did not mention to his father who would have ignored him. Felix went into a trance when he cooked. He shelled and chopped each pecan with precision, selected every raisin for its apparent succulence, and mercilessly discarded all of the imperfect. Looking upon their flaws with disgust, he wondered aloud what the world was coming to. "I don't know what those *cabrones* think. I'm no fool."

Who the *cabrones* were did not seem to matter and JoEl did not ask why they ruined the raisins. Evidently they were with the devil. "*Pobres cabrones*," he said with sympathy, and his father laughed long and loudly every time he remembered the story or told it to Christmas day visitors. Profanity from the mouth of a child never failed to assure him that innocence, if not perfect raisins, still existed in the world.

"*Pobres cabrones*," Felix said into his empty beer glass.

"What did you say?" The young soldier, fair with light-colored eyes, stood next to him while ordering another beer.

"*Cabrones?*" It's just an expression we Mexicans have. In English, you'd say something like 'poor bastards.'"

The boy did not respond. Instead, he ordered his beer with the cockiness of someone underage, almost daring the bartender not to serve him. Felix took to him immediately and offered to pay for it. The boy looked at him without smiling and thanked him in a sweet southern drawl.

"You're welcome," Felix said. "Where you from?"

"Tennessee."

The boy's voice and his guarded, tentative answers

excited Felix. He enjoyed making these shy types respond to his warmth. Even when they reacted in a surly or defensive manner, he did not give up the chase. They were his greatest challenge. Usually these encounters ended when he made them smile, talk, and even laugh openly at his bad jokes, their fear gone, their suspicions laid to rest. Once he had assured them that he was not interested in them for any perverse reason, they fell into his charming trap. Later, when he did make sexual allusions or even put his hand on their thighs while driving them to the base, they either responded according to their needs and desires or in embarrassed abrupt ways. Felix did not force them to do anything they did not want to do.

Most of all, he loved their youth and lack of guile. Even the most experienced among them had a certain purity that gravity, not worldliness, pulled down with the passing of time. They were in their prime, and when he was in their company and they permitted him to touch them, he tasted his own youth once again.

"How old are you?"

"Twenty-one." The boy was lying. Felix knew he could be no more than eighteen.

"What's your name?"

The boy told him and Felix observed that he had the mouth of a young girl. He had long since stopped wondering why his pursuit of the past led him to young men instead of women. He was secure in the love of his children, even when they quarreled with him, and he knew that Angie loved him. He was not looking for any of them in this boy's mouth. He was looking for something else.

"Can I give you a ride to the base?"

"Sure. Thank you very much," the boy replied with southern courtesy.

"It's just about sunset. Maybe we'll stop at the canyon on the way. It's nice there this time of day." The boy did not reply, and as Felix opened the door for them to walk out into the crisp winter light, he could smell the bright polish of the young soldier's boots.

It was one of his favorite times of year, the air clean and stinging his nose as they walked to the car. He had forgotten to phone his brother Miguel and ask for the money, but he would drop by tomorrow and talk to Juanita before Miguel got home. He usually visited his sister-in-law every Friday after work. They were fond of each other and he loved to make her laugh until tears came out of her small brown eyes.

Felix drove along the mountain so that he would not waste any time if the boy agreed to accompany him into the canyon. The eastern sunset was fine now, but the color would be gone by the time they got to his special place. Soon the March sandstorms would begin and the road would be closed. He detested those storms because they made him feel buried alive, and JoEl had learned not to tease him about his fear of them or the handkerchief he tied around his nose and mouth so that he would not smell the dust. He hated its bitter taste.

In the twilight there was no wind at all, and he was glad the young soldier did not smoke. They usually did. The sky was a bleached-out blue and the granite on that side of the mountain was a beige that made it difficult to distinguish planes and depths. A brilliant red-orange light outlined the edge of the mountain from the sun still setting on the other side. Off in the distance, toward the east, he saw the darkness coming at them.

"Ah don't think ah want to go into the canyon," the boy said.

"Oh, come on, only for a few minutes. It's real nice in there."

Felix took the boy's silence as an indication of consent and he began the slow drive up the canyon road. He maneuvered the car expertly, familiar with every turn and obstacle. They reached his secret place just as a soft quarter moon rose in the eastern horizon.

"Nice moon, isn't it?" Felix said and put his hand on the boy's knee. The boy sat rigidly on his side staring at the windshield and not the landscape. Felix sensed his preoccupation with the hand as it stroked his thigh.

"Don't do that," the boy said in a quiet, even tone.

"Don't be scared. I'm not going to hurt you. Let's have some . . . " The blows began before he finished. They were a complete surprise to him, and the anger behind them stunned and paralyzed him. He began to laugh as he warded off the attack, then stopped when the moon took on a strange shape and color.

"Hey, come on. I was just kidding." He was vaguely aware that he spoke through a mouthful of stones. It did not occur to him to struggle or to fight back. He forced his door open and fell to the ground, kicked sharply in the kidneys from behind. The stones in his mouth looked like teeth as he spat them out, and he turned to avoid the blows to his back. The boy stood over him. The kicking continued and he felt great pain in his groin and near his heart. Then his mouth was full of the desert and then it was not. He could no longer see the boy. The pain in his loins and along his side seemed distant, blotted out by a queer painful sensation in his left ear. He tasted the dust.

—Angie, where is my handkerchief? I hate this smell.

The biting ache in his ear began to recede and it seemed odd to be falling from a great height while lying on the desert floor. The sound of walking on stones puzzled him because he was surrounded by water. Its reflection and the luster of the boots flashed before him in an irregular, rhythmic motion. The beautiful youth was gone. Felix had time to be afraid before he heard his heart stop.

The desert exhaled as he sank into the water.

ANTS

Tia Cuca was lighter-skinned than her sister Chona. Nevertheless, like Mama Chona, she was unmistakably Mexican with enough Indian blood to give her those aristocratic cheekbones the two sisters liked the younger generation to believe were those of highborn Spanish ladies who just happened to find themselves in the provinces of Mexico. Their Spanish was a cultivated imitation of the Castilian Spanish they believed reigned supreme over all dialects, and they despaired that anyone in Miguel Chico's generation, because they were attending "American" schools, would ever master it. They were right.

Mama Chona and Tia Cuca were taught by nuns in Mexico before the 1910 revolution. If they did not approve of the language in which Miguel Chico and JoEl were learning to read and write, they did approve of the discipline under which they were instructed. "Listen to your teachers at school," Mama Chona told them in Spanish, "and learn to speak English the way they do. I speak it with an accent, so you must not imitate me. I will teach you how to speak Spanish properly for the family occasions."

Tia Cuca was more romantic about language. "Italian is the language of music," she said to the children in her lovely contralto voice. "French is the language of manners, English is the language of business, and Spanish—don't forget, children—is the language of love and romance." The only poetry she thought worth reading was that written in Spanish, "because it sings!"

Because of them Miguel Chico and his cousins learned to communicate in both languages fluently, a privilege denied the next generation, who began learning to read and write after Tia Cuca was dead and Mama Chona nearly senile. That generation understood Spanish but spoke it in ways that would have scandalized Mama Chona and her sister. "A truly educated person," Mama Chona told them, "speaks more than one language fluently."

The snobbery Mama Chona and Tia Cuca displayed in every way possible against the Indian and in favor of the Spanish in the Angels' blood was a constant puzzlement to most of the grandchildren. In subtle, persistent ways, family members were taught that only the Spanish side of their heritage was worth honoring and preserving; the Indian in them was pagan, servile, instinctive rather than intellectual, and was to be suppressed, its existence denied. Aunt Eduviges, Aunt Jesus Maria, and even Miguel Grande had learned this lesson well, taking to heart their mother's prejudices; Felix and Mema would have no part of it.

Miguel Chico's father practiced this kind of bigotry when he referred to the Mexican women who helped Juanita with the housework as "wetbacks." One of those "wetbacks" helped take care of Mama Chona in her last years with the devotion and humor of those saints who dedicate themselves to poverty.

"Is the Indian here yet?" Mama Chona would ask from the heights of her sickbed, even after she had forgotten most of her own children's names. "Tell her to do the dishes." The "Indian"—the last in a long line of distinguished women from across the border to be closely associated with the family—would say without sarcasm and with a wink at the children, "I've been here for several months, Señora Angel, and the dishes are already dry. Can I get you anything?" Having forgotten her question, Mama Chona would comment grouchily on the terrible accent of the illiterate masses.

Had she been alive in that period of Mama Chona's long act of dying, Tia Cuca would have joined her in criticizing the accent. She would not, however, have commented on any of the Indians' personal lives, no matter how often her sister asked her opinion of this or that girl who happened to be cleaning the house that year. Tia Cuca judged no one in matters of the heart.

Tia Cuca and Felix loved each other and were drawn together with the instinct of great sexual sinners. Like fat, contented cats, they enjoyed sharing a meal alone or in Mama Chona's company. Their frequent, unprovoked laughter would cause Mama Chona to ask, "What are you two up to now?" Since they were "up to" nothing, Tia Cuca, unable to resist teasing her puritanical sister, would answer, "You wouldn't understand, Chona; you've never understood anything about love." She meant "lust" and Chona knew it. Her defense was to ignore Cuca's comments except to indicate with a slight twitch of her nostrils that she had just caught the traces of a bad smell in the air. Tia Cuca and Felix laughed all the more.

Because his father was her favorite and because he was the youngest grandchild, JoEl spent more time in his childhood with Tia Cuca than did any of his older cousins or siblings, who had already served their periods of paying her their respects. He was frequently at Mama Chona's and thus it often fell to him to accompany her on the long bus ride to the house in the desert where Tia Cuca lived with a man named Davis. JoEl did not like these weekly visits, which were tediously the same, and he felt nothing for the old lady—an antipathy reinforced by his father's devotion to her.

JoEl and Mama Chona took the bus at ten in the morning when the weather was good, stayed for lunch, and returned by three to take their naps. For these visits, Mama Chona wore her formal black dress, put on black gloves, and carried her black umbrella. Puzzled, JoEl asked why she needed the umbrella, since rain fell only six or seven times a year in torrents that lasted but a few minutes. "I don't want the sun to burn my skin," she said. "It's dark enough already." JoEl looked closely at her very dark, leathery skin but asked no more questions. It was all a mystery, like her wearing even on the hottest days the black woolen dress that reached almost to the ground.

The mystery was enhanced by the atmosphere of sin that surrounded Tia Cuca's relationship with Mr. Davis. The old man, very white, tall, and skinny, reminded JoEl of a plucked pigeon, though he had a nice voice and a kind manner. Tia Cuca and Mr. Davis had lived together for as long as any of them, even his oldest cousins, could remember, and they remained together until they both died several weeks apart some time after JoEl's father was killed. Everyone knew they were lovers, but because Tia Cuca's explanations were deliberately evasive, no one knew if they had ever married. She always called him "Meester Davis," and he called her "Dolly."

Only JoEl's grandmother, his father, and his aunts Mema and Juanita visited Tia Cuca. Eduviges and Jesus Maria used their lack of transportation as an excuse for not going—they prayed for her daily and thus fulfilled their duty in a more spiritual way, they said—and Miguel Grande always spoke of her with contempt. Tia Cuca did not seem to care what anyone thought about her "arrangement" with Mr. Davis, and JoEl eventually came to feel a measure of respect for her. When she died she left modest sums—hardly more than six thousand dollars in all—to those members of the family who had always visited her. JoEl and Yerma each got five hundred dollars, which they understood was in memory of their father, though they were told it was to help pay for their music lessons.

JoEl remembered mostly the way she smelled. All little old ladies, even Mama Chona, seemed to have that rancid odor, like dried-up sticks. He did not like touching his great-aunt or his grandmother. When he had to give Tia Cuca a hug at their arrival and departure, he closed his eyes and held his breath. But she always embraced him long enough for him to have to breathe again and inhale her sour acacia mustiness. Then she gave him a nickel and told him to hide it somewhere. In that way, when he needed money, he would remember it and be wonderfully surprised. He never hid them. What good would nickels do him in the future? Such gifts were a great sacrifice for her, but he did not think of that. He bought his chiclets and chewed them.

His grandmother and her sister were the oldest human beings he knew, except for his mother's uncle Celso, who cut JoEl's hair every three weeks and smelled of lavender and Vitalis. Mama Chona and Tia Cuca must have been seventy and sixty-five respectively when he was born, though age was another mystery and no one ever said exactly how old they were at any given time, not even at their deaths. Rumor from his mother's side of the family calculated that Mama Chona was ninety-eight years old when she died, an estimation exaggerated to provoke Jesus Maria and Eduviges who had stopped counting after their forty-fifth birthdays. JoEl loved it when the grownups argued about their ages. As far as he was concerned, however, Mama Chona's life had ended when she could no longer remember the names of her children, much less those of their children.

On their visits, Mama Chona always warned him not to notice Tia Cuca's lame leg. But he loved to watch her use the black cane with the pewter handle, and later the crutches, with grandeur, as if they were extensions of herself. The two old ladies would soon settle down to talk, and their conversation, unimportant and for its own sake, after a while bored JoEl. When he grew restless he could on warm days play in the small yard within sight of the living room. On cold and windy days he was permitted to look at some of the picture books Tia Cuca had brought from Mexico. He enjoyed those books and was able to recognize some of the words Mama Chona had taught him in Spanish. Sometimes he would say them, and the two old ladies commented on his brilliance with bird-like sounds and exclamations, returning then to their conversation as if there had been no interruption.

The lunches at Tia Cuca's were not filling, and after each visit JoEl went straight to Mama Chona's icebox on the back porch. "I wish your father enjoyed eating here as much as you do, JoEl," Mama Chona said. "He goes to his aunt Cuca's more than to his own mother's. It pains me greatly." JoEl did not reply. He knew that his father was her favorite, and that when she called Felix a *malcriado*, she did so with affection.

Although they were always poor, the old ladies retained their aristocratic assumptions and remained señoras of the most pretentious sort. Their hands were never in dishwater, and cleaning house was work for the Indians, even if the old ladies could not afford to have them do it. Consequently, their homes were dusty, and his aunt Juanita or his father would do the weeks' collection of dishes. The only time JoEl saw Mama Chona lose her composure was when his uncle Miguel Grande scolded her for letting the cockroaches lick her plates clean on the sideboard. After his uncle left, Mama Chona held the plates one by one under the faucet in such a way that her fingers did not get wet, and she cried before, during, and after the loathsome task. JoEl's aunt Juanita, a meticulous housekeeper like his own mother, never could put up with his grandmother's ways.

Juanita seemed more tolerant of Tia Cuca's laziness, partly because she was lame and partly because the idea of cleaning up her place seemed hopeless, even to Juanita who would have gotten rid of the dust in the desert if she could. Until the day she died, no matter who threatened or cajoled her, Tia Cuca refused to do menial work. Her hands were small and exquisite and with great pride she said, "We may not have enough to eat, but when I go out, I put on my gloves and my hat. I am a civilized human being." She was secretly proud of having lighter skin than Mama Chona, and she made certain that the sun never touched her face and hands, the only parts of her any of them ever saw.

The succession of increasingly decrepit places Tia Cuca and Mister Davis rented, and later the house out in the desert beyond the canyon, were filled with cats. Tia Cuca fed them all—there might be ten to fifteen at a time—spoke to them by name (she gave them Spanish names like *Bella Luz, Sonrisa, Zapopan, Estrella,* and JoEl's favorite, *Platano*), and made certain that small entry doors at the front and back of the house were fixed to swing in both directions.

His aunt Juanita, terrified of cats, made JoEl laugh because of the way she sat at the edge of her chair when she visited. Tia Cuca murmured apologies, but the cats stayed, and he knew his aunt would be sick to her stomach when she got home. "Poor thing," Juanita said to his father, "I feel sorry for her, Felix, but those cats! They smell terrible and they make me sick."

JoEl and Mama Chona went regularly to the house in the desert for the first two years. But then he began to spend more time on his studies and with his friends, and his grandmother was beginning to get too old to make the trips. Only his father and his aunts Mema and Juanita continued to see Tia Cuca and after Felix died his aunts went less and less.

Following one period of two or three days when no one had been able to drive out, the mailman, at Tia Cuca's request, phoned Angie's house to inform the family that both old people were ill. Mema and Juanita then went every day to clean the house and change the linen, returning with stories that they shared with Angie in JoEl's presence. They had found the two old people unable to get up from their beds ("Imagine," said Juanita, "I always thought they slept in the same bed"), and because the desert had blocked up the cats' entrance the stench in the place was overwhelming. There were animals and cockroaches everywhere. The sheets were filthy.

Somehow Mr. Davis, breathing heavily but still conscious and lucid, had been able to feed them both during those days when they were completely alone. Tia Cuca, by the time her relatives arrived, was in a coma, and Mema soon insisted that she be taken to the hospital where she might die more comfortably. She asked Mr. Davis if he wanted to go also, lying that she would arrange for them to be in the same room. He knew he was dying; Mema was certain of that.

"No, Mema," he told her. "I know Dolly is going to die and I don't want to see her dead."

The day the ambulance made its way to what they all called "that shack" in the desert, Mema tried once again to get the old man to go along to the hospital. He refused and kept stroking Tia Cuca's hands and calling her "Dolly" until they took her away.

"Do you think she felt him touch her?" Yerma asked. JoEl did not want to hear Mema's answer but could not bring himself to leave the room.

"I doubt it," Mema said.

Mr. Davis died of pneumonia several weeks later in a different ward of the same hospital. No one told him that Tia Cuca was already dead and buried and he did not ask.

On one of his vacations home from school, JoEl drove his father's car out to the shack in the desert. He was beginning to look for touchstones that might release him from the terrible feelings he could only keep at bay with drugs. He drove into the canyon and stopped there for awhile, but he was too drunk to find his father's secret place. In the desert, the roof of Tia Cuca's house had been blown away and most of the windows were gone. Inside, everything was covered with sand and the ants were feeding on the carcasses of rodents. A few wild cats still roamed about, but JoEl did not touch them. Instead he sat on the back porch stairs for a long time, watching the sun set and playing a game with himself. In a notebook he always carried with him he wrote down all the names of Tia Cuca's cats that he could remember and then began making up riddles about them in Spanish and English. The game and the whiskey he had brought helped him forget about the ants inside the house.

A few days later, JoEl visited a friend on the southeast side of town near the lake. His mother had not allowed him to drive, so he took a bus. He got high with his friend and, not wanting to hitchhike home after dropping some acid, went to his aunt Eduviges' house a few blocks away. He had not been invited to stay with his friend because the parents did not like him and feared his bad influence over their son. "He's a worthless, drug-addicted Mexican, even though he has fair skin and goes to college. What a waste," they said. His family shared that opinion.

Eduviges' husband Sancho was away on a fishing trip and she was alone when JoEl arrived at her door at two-thirty in the morning. She had not seen her nephew for a long time and quickly noted his premature balding and his resemblance to Felix at that age.

"Is it all right if I stay here until morning?" he asked her. "I don't have a car and the buses have stopped running."

"Of course, JoEl, come in. Can I get you something to eat?" She was shocked at how old he looked.

"No, thank you, Tia. Please go back to bed. I'm sorry to disturb you at such an hour. I'm not sleepy. I'll just sit here on the sofa and read."

"No, that's fine, JoEl. I'll sit up with you. I'm not sleepy either." It was not true. She wanted to go back to bed more than anything else in the world, but she was afraid to leave him alone, was afraid of the look in his eyes. They had a sheen to them she did not trust, a fixed, dead, yet wild look that she associated with alcohol and sexual indulgence. She was very frightened. Her sister Jesus Maria, who lived a few blocks from Felix's house, had told her that JoEl had been visiting her lately and, with his head in her lap, weeping all the while, had complained that the family no longer loved him. When he wasn't in those desperate moods, Jesus Maria told her sister, JoEl talked about love and beauty very poetically and with a serenity that impressed her very much. Eduviges saw nothing serene in his look now. She thought him a lunatic.

The two of them sat in her living room in complete silence. They both would begin talking at once and then smile stupidly at each other. Eduviges knew that Angie would be furious if she found out that JoEl was with her. She looked at her nephew and remembered being told that after Felix was killed, JoEl had not allowed anyone to help him clean up the mess in the car. It was as if her brother's battered body were there in the house with her. She even imagined that JoEl, because of whatever drug he was on, might harm her, but because he was her brother's son she could not refuse him shelter.

"Mama Chona was talking to my father when she died," he said almost to himself, though loudly enough for Eduviges to hear.

She became terrified. "Sit still, JoEl, I'm going to the kitchen to heat up some *menudo* for us. Don't leave, I'll be right back." She recalled at the moment she was most afraid that JoEl had loved his father's cooking. Felix had taught her how to make the tripe soup.

Alone in his aunt's living room, JoEl stared through the tunnel that led him once again to the night of his father's death. He had not slept that night. The west wind was lifting the desert to their doorstep and March was a few weeks away. The sandstorms his father hated would begin soon. JoEl lay awake listening to the sand falling softly on the porch outside, a sound that made him think of veils sliding against each other or of the most delicate knives being sharpened—subtle, beautiful sounds which made him drowsy as he imagined each grain of sand falling.

Before going to bed he had asked Angie if Felix had taken a handkerchief with him. She did not remember. As he awaited his father's return, a terrible certainty made him open his mouth and swallow several times. It remained in his stomach heavy as a stone.

"Mamá, what time is it?"

"Eleven o'clock. Go to sleep. Your father will be here soon."

But his father was not coming home, and JoEl, struggling against his nightmare fears by not allowing himself to fall asleep, lay on his side and stared across the room at his father's bed. He felt no guilt about the morning quarrel. He knew it would resolve itself as all the others had. He felt only rocks in his belly, and his mouth was as dry as the veils and knives outside. He lay without moving for several hours until the heaviness left him as suddenly as it had come. He sat up and, leaning against the wall, continued to face his father's bed. Felix appeared to be there lying on his side, but JoEl could not see his face or hear the sound of his breathing. The wind had stopped.

In those moments, JoEl understood infinity for the first time. It was a region without dimensions which registered on one's consciousness in the same way that deaf mutes understand what others are saying to them. It was a timeless space where one is aware of movement without consequence, of a mouth uttering sounds one grasps but does not hear. All of his fears and evil dreams merged and he had no voice to cry out against them.

When Angie came in at five o'clock in the morning to tell him that someone was knocking on their front door, she thought he was in the middle of one of his nightmares. She did not touch him. "JoEl," she asked very gently, "are you all right?"

The sound of her voice brought him back. "Si, Mamá. Who's at the door?" He knew the answer.

"I don't know. Come with me."

They made their way through the house in the darkest hour of the morning without turning on lights or waking the others. Even Berto continued his innocent sleep on the sofa, despite the pounding. Before he unlocked the door, JoEl looked at his mother's lovely face in the growing light. He embraced her as he had after his childhood dreams. Angie felt his terror and his certainty, and as the knocking became more insistent she tried to stop JoEl from letting death come into her house.

"Who's there?" JoEl asked, turning the knob.

"It's Miguel. Open the door."

"It's Miguel. Open the door," JoEl said out loud.

"What did you say, JoEl?" Eduviges asked from the kitchen. "The *menudo* is ready. Why don't you come in here?"

Sitting down, he said matter-of-factly to her, "But it wasn't Miguel, auntie. It was death at the door." He was out of the tunnel and the aroma of the soup with hominy and squares of meat floating in it was a wonderland to devour.

"Of course, JoEl. Can you eat?" Eduviges asked.

Later that day, Angie phoned Mema who had just arrived home from her hospital volunteer work. JoEl was hysterical and had locked himself in the bathroom. He was ten years younger than her own son, and after Felix's death Mema had made a vow to herself to be responsible for JoEl.

Standing in the hallway of Angie's house, after asking Angie to leave her alone with him, Mema called to JoEl. By then, he had fallen silent and she was afraid he might have hurt himself.

"JoEl, it's Mema, please unlock the door and let me in. Please tell me you are all right."

He began shouting, "You're not Mema. You're death. Don't lie to me."

She was relieved. The silence had made her wonder how they would break the door down. "I can talk to a crazy man," she told Miguel Chico later, "but not to a dead one."

"Don't be silly, JoEl. It's your aunt Mema and your father wants me to talk to you." He opened the door.

"I like it that you were a whore once," JoEl told her. They were sitting on the floor, Mema leaning against the tub holding him. His head was on her shoulder, and she rocked him back and forth when she sensed that the drug he had taken was making him tremble.

"Well, I wasn't exactly. Your aunts like to exaggerate other people's mistakes."

"But you did what you wanted and you didn't care what they said."

"I was very young, JoEl. And I did care what my son might think if I found him."

"But you found him, and he's turned into such a prude, auntie. Just like Mama Chona, judging everybody." When on drugs, JoEl could tell the truth to everyone, even himself. "The ants are coming," he said and began to shake uncontrollably. Mema was strong enough to keep him from hurting himself.

"JoEl, I love Ricardo and I understand him," she said when the trembling had subsided. "Just as I love and understand you."

"No, you don't, Mema. No one in the family does any more, not even my mother."

"That's not true. The drugs make you say things like that."

"It's not the drugs. I don't know what it is, but it's not the drugs. I want," he stopped.

"What? What do you want? Tell me." She had been through this before with him and knew that it signaled the end of his journey.

"I want to see my father." He began choking. "I want to tell him that I understand and that I love him."

"He knows, JoEl."

"I want to tell him to his face. I hate it that Mama Chona is with him. She never understood anything human."

Mema remembered her own rage and desperation when Mama Chona initially agreed to take away her son. Time and circumstance had healed the wound, but the scar remained. "She did, JoEl, before she lost the people she loved very much. She just didn't know what to do without them. Maybe your father is giving her lessons now."

JoEl was nodding and could not keep his eyes open. She barely heard him ask her to stay. After a while, she called Angie and they carried him to bed.

Gradually JoEl began to speak to them only in riddles as if all the poetry once guiding him through his nightmares had itself turned into them. When Miguel Chico visited him in one of those halfway houses for the obsessed and addicted, JoEl would repeat everything his cousin said and giggle, then begin an endless monologue, his eyes daring Miguel Chico to interrupt him.

"JoEl, I have to go," he said.

"No, you don't. You're afraid of me. You hate the family and it loves you. I love the family and it hates me."

Miguel Chico stood. "No, it doesn't, JoEl. You don't know what you're talking about."

JoEl's eyes kept Mickie from touching him. "Please stop punishing yourself for what happened, JoEl," he said, but already JoEl had begun his litany, saying over and over again as Miguel Chico walked out of the room, "*Malcriado, malcriado, malcriado*, you've been bad, you've been bad, you've been bad." And then, even out in the hallway, Miguel Chico could hear him laughing and weeping simultaneously, "I love my father, I love my mother, I love my father, I love my mother."

THE RAIN GOD

Whered Miguel Chico returned to San Francisco after visiting his cousin in the desert, JoEl's words, like an incantation, kept waking him during the night and coloring his dreams in the greys and blacks and dark browns Mama Chona used to wear. In one of those dreams, the "monster" that had killed her said to him softly, almost kindly, "I am a nice monster. Come into my cave." The two of them were standing on a bridge facing the incoming fog. The monster held Miguel Chico closely from behind and whispered into his ear in a relentless, singsong way, "I am the manipulator and the manipulated." It put its velvet paw in Miguel Chico's hand and forced him to hold it tightly against his gut right below the appliance at his side. "I am the victim and slayer," the creature continued, "I am what you believe and what you don't believe, I am the loved and the unloved. I approve and turn away, I am judge and advocate." Miguel Chico wanted to escape but could not. The monster's breath smelled of fresh blood and feces. "You are in my cave, and you will do whatever I say." Although it moved away from him, Miguel Chico continued to feel its form pressed tightly against him, and the odor of its breath lingered, forcing him to gasp and struggle for air. The fog, he thought, would revive him and he thus kept his back to the monster and looked down and out at the sea no longer visible.

"Jump!" the monster said with exhilaration, "jump!"

Miguel Chico felt loathing and disgust for the beast. He turned to face it. Its eyes were swollen with tenderness. "All right," he said, "but I'm taking you with me." He clasped the monster to him—it did not struggle or complain—and threw both of them backward over the railing and into the fog. As he fell, the awful creature in his arms, Miguel Chico felt the pleasure of the avenged and an overwhelming relief.

Awakened by this dream in that silent hour before dawn when he felt the whole world was his, the sense of release was very much with him. This time he did not try to go back to sleep after changing his bag but instead sat at his desk and recorded the details of the dream. He needed very much to make peace with his dead, to prepare a feast for them so that they would stop haunting him. He would feed them words and make his candied skulls out of paper. He looked, once again, at that old photograph of himself and Mama Chona. The white daisies in her hat no longer frightened him; now that she was gone, the child in the picture held only a ghost by the hand and was free to tell the family secrets.

Before they went to the "American" schools, Mama Chona had instructed her favorite grandchildren almost daily, wanting to insure that they grew up according to her standards. *Malcriado* was her favorite word for a child, and to be called that by her was the worst form of censure, for it, meant that one was not only misbehaved, but that one had not been properly brought up. For a member of the Angel family, that was impossible. She taught them to love listening to and telling stories or *cuentos*, as she called them. When she was feeling gay, she treated them to comic book versions of the classics. Miguel Chico's favorite was *The Hunchback of Notre Dame* and he would look at it every night and pretend that he could read the words. He loved Esmeralda's name and a torture scene that featured a wooden boot, and he was simultaneously repelled and fascinated by Quasimodo.

Part of their instruction was to accompany Mama Chona on her visits to her sister and her daughters, where, she told them, they would learn proper manners. Also they would learn which buses to take and which streets were safe so that later when they were older, they might visit their aunts and cousins by themselves.

Mama Chona held Miguel Chico's hand tightly even when they stood waiting for the next bus, and she did not let go until they were safely inside his aunts' homes. Much of the children's knowledge of the family's history as well as its scandals came from those visits. Miguel Chico learned slowly that his aunts Jesus Maria and Eduviges exaggerated about the good and bad within the family chronicles, that Mama Chona preferred not to say much at all about their life in Mexico, and that only his aunt Mema told the truth. It was she who—while he was recovering from surgery—sent him the photograph of Mama Chona walking down the town's main street with him. "I don't know why," she wrote, "but I thought you might like to have this. I found it while sorting out that old chest of family photos and letters you used to love when you were a child." She also sent him a poem which she thought had been written out in longhand by the first

Miguel Angel in whose memory Miguel Chico and his father were named. The handwriting was beautiful, almost like calligraphy, and the poem a kind of prayer:

All the earth is a grave and nothing escapes it;
  nothing is so perfect that it does not descend
  to its tomb.
Rivers, rivulets, fountains and waters flow,
  but never return to their joyful beginnings;
  anxiously they hasten on to the vast realms
  of the Rain God.
As they widen their banks, they also fashion
  the sad urn of their burial.
Filled are the bowels of the earth
  with pestilential dust once flesh and bones,
  once animate bodies of men who sat upon thrones,
  decided cases, presided in council,
  commanded armies, conquered provinces,
  possessed treasure, destroyed temples,
  exulted in their pride, majesty, fortune,
  praise and power.
Vanished are these glories, just as the fearful smoke
  vanishes that belches forth from the infernal fires
  of Popocatepetl.

Nothing recalls them but the written page.
                    - Netzahualcoyotl
                      King of Texcoco
                      1431—1472

From Mema he had learned that the first Miguel Angel, Mama Chona's only child born of the love she had felt for her husband, was killed while walking down the streets of San Miguel de Allende at the beginning of the revolution that changed their lives and forced the family north from Mexico. A young and brilliant university student at the time, he was cut down by a single bullet while standing before the fountain he loved most on his way home from school. The friends who examined her son's body could not tell if the bullet lodged in his heart came from the government arsenal or from the camp of the revolutionaries. She did not care. Mama Chona never forgave Mexico for the death of her firstborn.

After they buried him, a delegation of revolutionaries came to her home in disguise while her husband Carlos was away to tell her they considered her son a hero. She looked at them in rage and disbelief. "Keep your hero," she said to them at the door, "give me back my son." Soon after, a letter from the general in command of the federal forces in that region praised her son for being a true patriot on the side of honor and right. The president's seal was affixed to it and she was encouraged to believe that he had signed it personally. Her husband kept the letter and it became the accepted version of the first Miguel Angel's death. Mama Chona did not care which version was told. She detested the pomposity of men at war and blamed both pro- and anti-government forces for the murder of her son.

"Just remember to have respect for your parents," Mama Chona told Miguel Chico and his cousins in her beautiful Spanish, "and everything will be all right." She said little to them about herself; she taught and admonished them. "And be careful always when you are outside of your house and away from your family." No harm, Mama Chona made them believe, could ever come from within one's own home and family.

Eight years before her first child was killed, Mama

Chona's twin girls had died. They drowned in those few moments when one of the servants let down her guard. Mama Chona taught her children to be careful and they died because they would not mind her or what they were doing. In her world, there were no accidents. Every event was divine retribution or blessing. After the deaths of her first three children, Mama Chona resigned herself to Christ and His holy Mother with a fervor she would never have admitted was born of rage, and she accepted suffering in this life without question or any sense of rebellion. She renounced all joy on the day they buried Miguel. She was thirty-two.

From then on, Mama Chona bore her children out of duty to her husband and the Church. Thinking that after a stillborn child she might be barren, she was disappointed when she gave birth to Felix. In her mind, she conceived him and the rest immaculately—an attitude which made some of her children think themselves divine—blotting out the act which caused her to become distended like a pig bladder full of air. Later in her life, in that time when Miguel Chico and JoEl fell under her instruction, Mama Chona denied the existence of all parts of the body below the neck, with the exception of her hands. They were her only feature that rivaled her sister Cuca's in beauty.

"God forgive me," she said in her grandchildren's presence. "What beautiful hands I have," and she extended them, palms down, so that they might admire without touching. Mama Chona was not physically affectionate. Touching other people reminded her of her own body, and she encouraged her grandchildren to develop their minds, which were infinitely more precious and closer to God. She had given up on her own children.

Felix, Jesus Maria, Eduviges, Armando, Mema, and Miguel Grande—dreamers and lechers were all she managed to produce. God was testing her, she knew, by having sent her such intractable souls to nourish alone in a desert far from the green and tropical place of her birth. Her husband died in 1916, two months before her last child was born, as they traveled north toward the desert.

The first family scandal Miguel Chico was old enough to be aware of involved his aunt Mema. Before he was born, Mema had an illegitimate child and the family had decided that she must give him up. In protest, Mema went to live across the river with her man, which in her sisters' eyes was the same as becoming a woman of the streets. Mema did not care what they thought. She considered them pious hypocrites and she was determined to bring her son back into the family.

Six years later she found him, wandering the streets of Juarez, shining shoes and begging for his living. He had run away from the home where he had been placed and he accepted Mema's kindness at first more than her story. Her brother Felix persuaded Mama Chona to bring him back into the family legally. And so Ricardo, the bastard child, became the adopted son of his grandmother and uncle, a puzzling arrangement which the many cousins he acquired instantly were not allowed to discuss. Miguel Chico was three or four years younger than Mema's son.

Mema knew she could not afford to keep him with her, and she wanted Ricardo to be educated and brought up on the north side of the river. Mama Chona readily assented to the adoption because she saw it as a way to get her daughter away from her sinful life and back into the family. But Mema refused to accompany her son and stubbornly remained with her man. She visited Ricardo and Mama Chona regularly and brought the boy gifts paid for by any extra money she was able to set aside.

Mama Chona's sister Cuca defended Mema's choice. "You don't know anything about love," Cuca said to her. "You never have."

"Don't talk to me about love. I don't see that you've had any children, Cuca. What do you know about it except your romantic notions that can't sustain and feed a family? You mean lust, Cuca. Every one of my children has been ruined by it and you have not been a good example to them."

"I can't talk about love to anyone who doesn't know about it," Cuca said and ended the discussion.

So Mema's son Ricardo came to live with Mama Chona in a two-room *casita* that Miguel Grande built for them in the backyard of the two-bedroom house he and Juanita had just moved into. It was the first house they owned. Mama Chona treated Ricardo kindly, even with some affection, and she did not expect of him the kind of perfection she demanded of her own children and grandchildren. Whenever he had the slightest illness, she took care of him and fed him sugar water with *canela*. As she taught Miguel Chico to read in Spanish, she taught Ricardo English. In them and later in JoEl, she saw an intelligence worth cultivating.

By teaching Ricardo, she would also teach her daughter Jesus Maria a lesson. Jesus Maria had severely disappointed Mama Chona by marrying against her wishes. And from the moment she had learned of the plan to adopt the bastard child she had argued vehemently against it. "But Mamá," Jesus Maria began in the elegant Spanish she had learned from Mama Chona, "how can you let that child live with you when you know from what sin he comes?"

Mama Chona and Miguel Chico were sitting in Jesus Maria's dark, musty parlor. The shades were drawn in the summer to keep out the heat, and in the winter to keep it in. Mama Chona watched her daughter in silence, knowing that her indifference angered Jesus Maria and that she could in this way win every argument because she could always say, as she invariably did, that no one who was shrieking at her could possibly be in her right mind about any given subject. Jesus Maria, in tears and carried away by her own drama and the pitiable state of her life—which she never failed to describe in detail at all hours to her husband and children— would stop shouting, stunned by the injustice of having to deal with such an unsympathetic mother. Mama Chona would already be out the door and halfway to the bus stop with Miguel Chico by her side before Jesus Maria realized that once again she had been defeated. But not before she could complain about her mother's unfairness.

"Mamá, you have never loved me, I who have been a good and dutiful daughter, except in marrying against your wishes. But at least I married before I had my children, as you and the Church taught me was not only proper but necessary to remain in a state of grace." Jesus Maria attended mass daily. "You were right about my husband. He is uneducated, coarse, but he is a good worker and he makes enough money at a decent job to feed me and the children and keep a roof over our heads." She had married Manuel Chavez because he was handsome and had flattered her with his attention. "Every day of their lives, I teach my children not to be like their father, but to aspire to greater things and to that perfection you and the Church have taught me is the only worthy goal in life. He is ill mannered, but my sons and daughters are not. His speech is faulty, my children speak like angels. You have never appreciated them enough, Mamá. Now you tell me that Mema's bastard is going to live with you as your son. I cannot believe it. It was a scandal that he was born. You, you, Mamá, agreed when we first discussed it to put him up for adoption. I had to go to the agency and fill out the papers and I have never felt so humiliated in my life. But I did it because the others were too weak and sentimental to see that it had to be done if we were going to retain any pride in this family. Now I think I should have murdered him, God forgive me."

Mama Chona shifted in her chair. Only Miguel Chico, standing next to her and leaning on its arm, felt her move like the smallest of earthquakes. "Jesus Maria," she said, "you don't mean that. You are in such a state that you don't know what you are saying." She marveled at the duplicity of her daughter, who had just returned from taking Jesus to her soul and yet spoke of slaughtering innocents.

"Yes, I do know what I'm saying and I am not in any 'state.' You have never loved me as much as Mema, who betrayed you much worse than I ever have or could possibly think of doing. But no, when it comes to your favorites, you have no eyes, no ears, no voice to see that they are wrong and that you must deny them what they want. You have always loved them more." Jesus Maria patted her face delicately with her handkerchief, folded her hands, and looked at her mother with swollen eyes. "Mamá, if you let that bastard live with you, I will not enter your house. And if you bring him here, I will not open the door to you. These things are very hard for me to say because you are my mother and I must respect you above all others on earth, but I will not stand for this insult to the family, do you hear me?" Throughout her life, Jesus Maria thought of herself as an Angel, never as a Chavez.

"The way you are shouting, Jesus Maria," Mama Chona replied calmly and firmly, "the entire neighborhood can hear you." She paused. "I have also taught you to love your brothers and sisters as yourself and to forgive them when they do wrong. Don't you see that it was a miracle that Mema found her son after we allowed him to be taken away from her? It is a sign from God that we must bring him back into the family. You are too proud, Jesus Maria, and God will punish you for that. I forgive you for shouting at me, your mother, and for going against my wishes, but how can He?"

Wrapped in her shawl, even on the hottest days, her umbrella ready for the rays of the desert sun, Mama Chona made her way to the corner to wait for the bus. She knew that Jesus Maria would agonize over having been a disobedient child. She knew also that Jesus Maria's pride would not permit her to invite her mother to wait inside until the bus could be heard. In that way, she trapped her daughter's objections to the adoption of Ricardo between pride and guilt. Mama Chona had learned well the lessons the nuns taught.

"I hear the bus, Mama Chona," Miguel Chico said after they had been waiting in the sun long enough for him to see the wavy lines that made him think the whole world was underwater. Her umbrella was not large enough to shelter him and there were no trees.

"Do you want to go downtown?" she asked him in Spanish.

"Oh, yes, please." He did not like to visit Jesus Maria's house because his cousins made fun of his ears and accused him of being a sissy. Going downtown would help him forget their taunts. Miguel Chico took her hand and helped her into the bus.

"*Gracias*, Miguelito," she said after he found a place for them to sit near the front of the bus. She had taught him to avoid the rear, which was labeled the "colored section." Once, before he understood what such labels meant, he had

169

rushed to a seat in the back so that they would not have to stand in the aisle. Mama Chona had wrenched him out of it, and they had stood all the way to their destination. "No one should sit there," she told him and his cousins. "It's an outrage."

Mama Chona and Miguel Chico got off the bus at the downtown plaza. A small, pretentious and ugly fountain stood in the middle of the square, and the town paid hundreds of dollars a year to feed and maintain the pathetic alligators lying inert around it.

"They've ruined this plaza," Mama Chona said. "You should have seen it years ago, Miguelito." There was a rare tone of affection in her voice, and she was looking at him strangely. "There is a fountain in San Miguel de Allende," she added, then stopped. He did not understand. Mama Chona took his hand, as she always did when they were among strangers. No one was going to shoot this child in the streets.

After her eightieth birthday, Mama Chona returned to her girlhood more often. She conquered time by denying its existence, and Mema would find her awake or asleep at odd hours of the day and night. Miguel Grande and his brothers-in-law had put enough money together to rent a small apartment, and Mema, now in her fifties, left her life across the river and came to live with her mother. Mama Chona was no longer able to care for herself and the family would not think of putting her in a nursing home.

Miguel Grande visited his mother nearly every day

during her last ten years; Jesus Maria and Eduviges phoned often but seldom visited. They spoke civilly, even nicely, to their fallen sister whose assault on the family pride, more than her unforgivable sin, had wounded them deeply. That pride never seemed affected by time either.

Even the seasons—"In the desert, there are two seasons," Mama Chona told them, "very hot and very cold"—no longer touched the old lady. On several occasions, Mema found her mother outside without her shawl on icy days, watering the flower beds.

"Mamá, what are you doing?"

"Taking care of the flowers. Without me, everything would die."

Another time, she startled JoEl in the dead of winter by saying, "Listen to the crickets, Felix, what a noise they make." The grandchildren no longer attempted to correct her when she confused them with their parents. Mama Chona's face took on a diabolical sheen in those moments and JoEl, the initial shock of his own confrontation with time worn off, learned to ignore her. He looked out the window. The land and the sky were the same texture and the day was soundless.

The family talk was now filled with stories about her strange behavior and conversation, and until the bath incident everyone regarded them with tolerance and amusement. Mema reported that Mama Chona now woke up in the middle of the night and wandered through the apartment searching for something.

"Mamá, what are you looking for?"

Mama Chona spoke only to herself, even as her daughter held her to keep her from falling in the darkness. She did reply once to Mema's question, "I am looking for my children." More often, she would mumble unintelligibly, as if she were saying the rosary or reciting a school lesson learned by rote for the nuns.

In the daytime, usually before the late afternoon meal, she would ask, "Where is your father?" The first time she asked, Mema, surprised, told her straight-forwardly that he was dead. Without blinking, Chona retorted, "Yes, but why doesn't he come to see me? Where is he?"

Another day, sitting in the parlor waiting for a sandstorm to blow over, Mama Chona said very seriously to Mema, "I saw your father today. He was with that woman Josefina. They came to see me together, can you imagine? I knew he was seeing a great deal of her, but it was shameless of him to bring her here when there are children in the house. I will not forgive him for that." It was the first any of them had heard of Josefina—Mama Chona had always told them what a respectable and upright man their father Carlos was—and Mema wanted to find out more but dared not ask.

Gradually it became more and more dangerous to let Mama Chona out of their sight, even for a few moments. One day when Mema had let down her guard, her mother wandered out of the house and Mema and Miguel Grande spent hours looking for her. They found her standing on the corner of one of the busiest intersections in the downtown shopping district, facing toward Mexico and waving cars to the curb in order to ask the startled passengers if they knew where her husband was. After that she was watched constantly by her children or grandchildren, and, on holidays, by the Mexican women they hired from across the border.

Miguel Grande and Mema often joked with each other in their mother's presence as a way of coping with her disintegration. After one of Miguel Grande's visits, Mama Chona asked, "Who was that chap? I like him very much."

When Mema reported that to him, they laughed with delight. Jesus Maria, however, was appalled by her mother's fading memory and refused to be taken in by the others' gross and flippant views of such a tragedy. She no longer dealt with her mother directly, preferring the distance of a phone call. Out of perversity, Mema would always ask Mama Chona if she wished to speak to Jesus Maria before she hung up.

"I don't know any Jesus Maria," Mama Chona said. "Who are you talking about? One of your friends from Juarez? Leave me alone, *malcriada*."

Mema repeated the answer to her sister. They both understood that when Mama Chona referred to Mema's "friends" from across the river, she meant prostitutes, and the inference caused Jesus Maria to rage for the rest of the day. Even in her witlessness, she said to her children and nephews, their grandmother found ways to taunt her and make life more miserable than it already was for all of them. Nonetheless, she was quick to add, they must respect Mama Chona and continue to pray for her health. She herself must learn to bear her cross with joy. Bearing crosses, the children knew, was her favorite pastime.

Five years later, Encarnacion Olmeca *viuda de* Angel looked for the last time at all her children and their children. She asked that she be raised up so that she might see their faces, and Miguel Grande and Mema propped pillows behind her while Ricardo, now in his twenties, held her hands tenderly. It was strange to her that he, the scandal of the family, was the one who comforted her most in her long and painless act of dying. There was no doubt in her soul that at last she was to leave the desert of thorns and ashes in which she had lived most of her life.

Miguel Grande, who in the last few years had scolded

her a great deal for growing old, broke down as he held her. Mama Chona was as weightless as a lizard dried hollow by the sun.

—Crybaby, Miguel, you were always the most sentimental in this family. You never fooled me.

If she had not felt them touching her, Mama Chona would have floated straight to heaven where she was certain of admission. How could the heavenly hosts turn her away? It was the moment she had been waiting for all her life, a life of loss and sacrifice. Her husband and five of her children had been taken from her and she had suffered enough from the conduct of the survivors to be canonized. If there was justice in heaven, as she knew there was not on earth, the angels were preparing to welcome her with songs and jewels in their hands as offerings for the scars on her soul. Music and beautiful things had been her secret passions.

She had not believed them when they told her that Felix was dead also, killed in an accident at the factory. He was only being his silly, irresponsible self, visiting Cuca instead of her because his aunt was more entertaining and had lighter skin. *Malcriado!* She knew him. He was nothing but a gadabout and as worthless as the rest of her children. Who would worry over their souls after she was gone?

Eduviges had betrayed her in the last month by making her take a bath. Mama Chona had known for some time what her children were up to in their lifelong plan to torment her. First they wished to shame her and then to poison her with the bath water. She had not left the apartment or bathed for weeks, from the moment she had noticed something unnatural coming out of her womb. "Another worthless creature," she said to her husband Carlos who had taken to visiting her, "you ought to be ashamed of yourself." By not allowing herself to be naked, she had successfully denied the existence of the monster. She lost her temper the day Eduviges made preparations to get her into the tub.

"Mamá, I'm going to bathe you," she said.

"No. I don't want a bath. Leave me alone, please."

"But, Mamá, you haven't had a bath in a long time. What's the matter? Are you afraid?"

"I'm not afraid. I know what you and Mema are doing. You want to poison me. You've never had any respect for me, *malcriadas*, and now you want to kill me. Well, I'm still the head of this family and I won't let you."

This was too much for Eduviges, who prided herself on being Mama Chona's most obedient, least bothersome child. To be accused of wanting to murder her own mother was the final insult. But Mema had warned her, and now she had to clutch Mama Chona by the arm and lead her forcibly—they were the same size—into the bathroom. The water was drawn and steaming, and the clean, perfumed towels lay waiting in neat piles. Eduviges had worked very hard to make the ordeal appealing.

"Take off your clothes," she ordered with as much menace as she could find in her heart for the old lady. Mama Chona grabbed the towels and threw them into the water with unexpected quickness, screamed that her daughter was poisoning her, struggled wildly, and scratched Eduviges' cheek. She slapped Mama Chona and sat her down on the toilet seat. "If you don't stay right here until I come back, Mamá, I will kill you," she said. She ran down the hall to phone Miguel, the only member of the family who could make their mother obey. It was just after six in the morning.

Miguel Grande, awakened by her call, could not make out what his sister was shouting about. Hysterical women made him more impatient than anything else in the world.

"What the hell is going on? It's six o'clock and Sunday morning."

"I know what time it is," she screamed.

"Calm down and tell me what's going on."

After he understood, he told Juanita to get up and the two of them drove across town to his sister's house. Sancho was away on a hunting trip, not wanting to be involved in the plot to bathe his mother-in-law.

When Miguel and Juanita walked into the bathroom, Eduviges and Mema were holding Mama Chona and Miguel Grande was amused by his mother's fighting spirit. He had no idea the old woman had that much strength left in her.

"Mamá!" he shouted. "Be still!"

He yelled ferociously at her, knowing from their experiences with her in the last two years that this made her calm and submissive. The first time he had used this tone with her, Juanita had wept at the disrespect and violence he was showing his mother. She had not cared much for Mama Chona, but she did not like to see anyone treated like a criminal.

Encarnacion quieted down and stared at her husband, her eyes wide and shining with a scorpion's fury. Her breath came in short, wheezing noises, and she was fighting to force her soul out of her body. In a harsh, loud, and steady voice, her husband was telling her that as soon as he left the bathroom, the women were going to undress her and give her a bath. That if she refused to let them do so, he would do it himself. That he was ashamed of a woman who allowed herself to become so unclean that her odor was unpleasant to the people who loved and respected her. That she was being foolish and behaving like a child, and that if she continued to misbehave, he would commit her to a hospital and order the doctors and nurses there to clean her up.

"Sí, Carlos," she said, assenting like the child her husband always made her feel she was.

In a chair outside the bathroom door, sipping the instant coffee he had made for himself and reading the newspaper, Miguel Grande heard soft splashing sounds and a quiet conversation between his sisters and his wife that he did not heed. He grinned to himself, the image of his mother about to take a swing at his sister Eduviges still before him. "What a woman," he said affectionately into his coffee cup, wondering why his mother had begun calling him by their father's name. Juanita came out first, her clothes drenched and her face sweaty from the steam. She was as pale as if she were going to be sick. "What's wrong?" he asked her. "What's the matter now?"

"Miguel, call Dr. Ahrens right away. Your mother is very ill. Her uterus is falling out and she's bleeding a lot."

The monster between her legs was almost out and Mama Chona was glad that it showed no signs of life. All the better for it. It had not bothered her and she did not understand why everyone else was making such a fuss over it. One should ignore those parts of the body anyway. Filthy children, all they ever thought about was the body.

Propped up in a strange bed in an unfamiliar and sterile room, Mama Chona saw her children around her, weeping quietly. Even their husbands and wives were with them. They were inundating her with their grief, which she considered false and silly. She wanted them to go away and let her die in peace and she pretended to sleep, hoping they would leave.

Ricardo was holding her hands still and she did not have the strength to push him away. He spoke softly to her in Spanish, telling her who was in the room in a voice that was pleasing to her.

—Ricardo, you are a good boy. But how can I leave the family to you, the bastard son?

"Mamá," he said to her, his head almost next to hers on the pillow. "We are all here. Your sons and daughters, your grandsons and granddaughters, all the family. You gave us life and we will make you proud of us after you have gone to heaven. We respect and love you very much. You need not be afraid."

—Afraid? Afraid of what? She had known death all her life. Her existence had been a long dying fall. She welcomed death. Even in her imperfection, she knew that Jesus and His Mother would take her to them and comfort her for all eternity. He, at least, was a good son, though sometimes she had had her doubts when she thought about the suffering He had caused His Mother. Mary, children aren't worth the trouble. Sweet and loving as babies, they turn into monsters who cast you aside and compete with one another to see which of them can cause you the most pain. Your Son alone was worth the trouble, but He made you suffer a great deal. Still, He made you queen of heaven. But my children, mother of God, have not been worth the trouble.

"What did you say, Mamá?" Jesus Maria asked. They had all taken turns saying a few words to her at the bedside. She was the last. "Mamá, it's Jesus Maria. Can you hear me?"

—Jesus Maria! the child she had named for her beloved Jesus and Mary.

"Mamá, forgive me." Jesus Maria, allowing herself to weep in front of her mother for the last time, choked out her apologies and sang the litany of the disobedient child. Even Miguel Grande, usually contemptuous of his sister's hypocrisy, felt moved and looked with some pity at her humiliation before the family. Jesus Maria, carried away with her performance, took advantage of the allotted time and chided herself publicly for having been a trial to the poor mother now lying defenselessly before their eyes.

Mama Chona opened her eyes and looked at her daughter with full recognition. "It's about time," she said for all to hear and closed her eyes once more. Jesus Maria stopped crying instantly and retreated to her husband's side.

Days passed during which Mama Chona heard and smelled rainstorms passing over the desert. She longed to see the yucca and ocotillo in bloom, to breathe in their fragrance and praise them for their thorniness and endurance. If only human beings could be like plants. In one of her daydreams, she saw the desert sand filled with verbenas and blooming dandelions, and with the first Miguel by her side, she discovered wild roses. The mourning doves accompanying them were the color of twilight. "Look," she said to her son, "look!" She opened her eyes and saw that she was still in that strange room with all the family waiting for her to die.

—Why do they weep? Why don't they go away? I'll speak to them.

"Children," she said, after Mema helped her take a few sips of water, "children, don't weep. I am happy to leave this valley of tears because I know the life awaiting me will be much, much better. Please don't cry any more. Leave me in peace with Jesus and His Holy Mother."

Slowly, the weeping noises subsided and the room became completely silent. After a few moments, Mama Chona opened her eyes abruptly. Mema later swore she heard them click. The old woman looked at them for the last time.

Even Felix had finally come to visit her. He was standing between Miguel Chico and JoEl. She reached out to them but was unable to lift her arms.

Miguel Chico felt the Rain God come into the room.

—Let go of my hand, Mama Chona. I don't want to die.

"*La familia,*" she said.

Felix walked toward her out of the shadows. "Mamá," he called in a child's voice that startled her.

"All right," she said to the living in the room, "if you want to, you can cry a little bit."

To Felix, she said, "Where have you been, *malcriado?*" He took her in his arms. He smelled like the desert after a rainstorm.